"Dad," I

He turned around and his expression was a study in wonder. He gestured to the world outside. "You know, life is really beautiful."

I went over to the window, stood next to him. More light flooded the room, us, the yard.

"It is, isn't it?"

"I'd forgotten how really wonderful life is."

"Most mornings I come out here and take a few minutes to enjoy it."

"You're a smart girl." He stared at me for a moment. "I was just thinking how much I've missed. I was always working." He sighs. "Trying to make buildings perfect." He glances out to the yard again. "But life doesn't have to be perfect, does it?"

"Maybe our flaws are beautiful, too." I think about this, hope it's true, feel good that we're talking. We both stare at the yard and, suddenly, it turns bright with sunlight.

Mary Schramski

Mary Schramski began writing when she was about ten. The first story she wrote took place at a junior high school. Her mother told her it was good, so she immediately threw it away. She read F. Scott Fitzgerald at eleven, fell in love with storytelling and decided to teach English. She holds a Ph.D in creative writing and enjoys teaching and encouraging other writers. She lives in Nevada with her husband, and her daughter who lives close by. Visit Mary's Web site at www.maryschramski.com.

Falling Out *of* Bed
Mary Schramski

FALLING OUT OF BED

copyright © 2006 Mary L. Schramski

isbn 037388091X

TheNextNovel.com

 HARLEQUIN®

PRINTED IN U.S.A.

From the Author

Dear Reader,

The idea for *Falling Out of Bed* came to me through a conversation with a dear friend. Over cups of tea we talked about what we thought to be important in our lives, and how those ideals guide us. After our conversation, I began imagining a character struggling with what she believed in and how her family might help her evolve. Melinda is the brave protagonist in *Falling Out of Bed*, the one who learns about love, hope and believing in things she cannot explain.

Sincerely,

Mary Schramski

www.maryschramski.com

To you, the reader

If winter comes, can spring be far behind?
—Percy Bysshe Shelley

Even the seasons form a great circle in their changing, and always come back again to where they were. The life of a man [woman] is a circle from childhood to childhood and so it is in everything where power moves.
—Black Elk

PROLOGUE

Second Week in October

I'm on my knees by the oak tree. For my forty-second birthday my father sent me fifteen daffodil bulbs from a mail-order catalog. I don't garden, so after I opened his gift I walked down to Elizabeth's house and asked her how to plant them.

She smiled, patted my shoulder. "Dig really deep, Melinda. Then wait for miracles to appear in the spring."

I looked at the bulbs. "All that from daffodils?"

"Oh, they're more than that. They prove there's always hope." Then she reached inside the box, touched one of the rough woodlike seeds and looked at me. "We all need hope."

I shook my head, laughed. "I guess you're right, but my life's pretty wonderful right now. I'm not sure why my father sent me these. Maybe I'll find out someday." I closed the box, gave her a hug and walked home.

The telling autumn breeze washes over me and I stare at the daffodil bulb in my palm. The tiny orb looks so dark against my skin. How can something so hard and ugly produce a delicate flower?

CHAPTER ONE

First Week in January

"Dad's back still hurts," I say as I walk into our family room. My husband is sitting in his recliner watching TV and canned laughter fills the room.

David looks at me. "It's probably just a pulled muscle. Your father's healthy as a horse. He'll be fine."

"I know." Deep down I'm not sure this is true, but I press my lips together, tell myself not to worry. At seventy-two years old, Dad's a health nut, a runner, a person who is never sick.

David turns his attention back to the TV. The huge Sony big-screen, the actors and the fake laughter have taken over our living room as they do most nights. The woman on TV is having a baby and the entire family—husband, children and mother-in-law—are in an uproar, worried and nervous for her.

Our lives, on the other hand, are easy. Our only child is doing well in college, by choice I haven't worked in over a year, and David is happy. I taught junior high for eighteen years, but I quit because I was bored and dreaded going in each day. We didn't need the money and now I spend my time volunteering at the library, thinking about what I'd like to do when I go back to work, and keeping our house immaculate.

David, in the TV's shimmery light, looks rested from our uneventful weekend. He laughs again and the sound echoes against the ten-foot ceilings of our home. My husband loves TV. He always has. When we were first married, I asked him why he watched so much. He explained that watching TV was the only thing to do while his mother worked nights.

This was the opposite of what I experienced. When I was growing up, before my mother and father divorced, the four of us sat in our living room, listened to music and read.

I guess parts of our childhoods stay with us forever.

For a moment, there is a square of silence before another TV commercial comes on. I hear the winter wind moving outside. It is extremely cold tonight and for some silly reason I think about the daffodil bulbs I planted months ago and wonder if they are all right.

I lie back on the couch, pull the soft beige Pottery Barn throw over my legs and open the book I was reading before Dad called. Yet the feeling my father's backache is something more slips around me like a silk curtain.

Every once in a while I experience a weird intuition I can't deny. These intuitive feelings aren't anything supernatural or scary, but since I was about eight, some things turn out exactly the way I know they will. When this happens I always feel uncomfortable.

The most poignant one was the time when I was eight months pregnant. I dreamed about our unborn daughter Jennifer. I saw her dark thatch of hair, her beautiful slanted eyes and cupid lips. That morning, right after I woke, while David was still sleeping and sunlight sprang into the bedroom, I had no doubt our child would be a girl. And I was overjoyed even though David was hoping for a boy. Our daughter was born with the beautiful little face, the one that appeared in my dream.

Women seem to understand this story better than men. When I tell a woman about my *Jennifer dream*, she usually nods and smiles. Men don't. David thought my dream was a coincidence. But I knew it wasn't. And I tried to explain to him how I felt like a fraud and guilty about my best friend Vanessa's death. How I couldn't stop wondering why, if I have this intuition, I didn't know my college roommate shouldn't have gone for a ride with her boyfriend the night their car overturned.

David always says to forget all that. But it's not that easy.

I've explained to Elizabeth about my intuition and she claims it's a gift from God. Elizabeth and I are different in that way—she has a strong faith, I don't. Before Vanessa's death I believed there was some sort of God and maybe a plan for us all. But after, it was like someone took a rag and wiped my beliefs away. Now I think life is just a big petri dish.

David laughs again, looks over at me. "That was funny."

"Sorry, I wasn't watching."

"Your Dad's gonna be okay, Melinda. Quit worrying."

"I know." I smile and he smiles back, but at this moment, underneath my happy facade, I know our lives will never be the same.

* * *

My father and I are talking on the phone again.

I'm determined to cheer him up. Last night I left
David to his TV shows and went to bed early. This
morning I woke feeling better, upbeat. Beautiful
winter sun was blazing into each room of our home
and I thought, *Of course Dad will be fine.* Before I
could phone him, my mother called and I told her
about Dad's backache.

"Stanley has always been strong as an ox. He's
flawless, and if he isn't, he'll make himself that way.
Don't worry, he'll survive," she said.

Her words of encouragement made me feel even
better.

"I know I'll be okay, honey," Dad says through the
phone line. "But my back sure hurts."

"Does Motrin help?" I'm happy I can give him
moral support and a little advice. We aren't close
and I've always wanted to be.

"No."

"The doctors in El Paso will fix you up. Once you
get their diagnosis, you'll be better."

Dad is going to an orthopedic surgeon this afternoon in El Paso, fifty miles from Las Cruces, New
Mexico, where he lives. I wish we lived closer so I

could drive him to the doctor. He and I see each other maybe once every three years. The last few years since his retirement, we've talked more on the phone and it's nice. But this morning Grapevine, Texas, seems very far away from Las Cruces.

"Maybe today the doctors will have an answer," he says.

"Of course. Call me when you get back with the good news."

We say goodbye. I walk into the living room where there is a mélange of family photos on the wall. I study the photo of my mother and Dad before they divorced—smiling, standing close. Then my gaze settles on a worn black-and-white picture—my father at six months—staring into the camera with a look of baby surprise. His thatch of dark hair and slightly slanted eyes remind me of my daughter Jennifer.

I touch the glass with my right index finger, hope I don't leave a smudge.

Of course you'll be okay.

Of course.

For nine hours, David and I have been speeding down ribbons of Texas and New Mexico highways in my blue Toyota Camry. He is driving and I have asked him three times not to go over seventy-five but he won't slow down. A little while ago I gave up trying to save our lives. Instead I got my stack of magazines from the back seat and began flipping through the glossy pages in an effort to not worry about my father.

The car slows and I look up. We turn off the freeway—the El Paso Exit 7. I sigh. We are here to lend moral support to my father who was diagnosed with bone cancer three days ago. When Dad informed me of what the doctors had found, I told him I would drive to El Paso to be with him, help him. He didn't say, *No, don't come*, but wondered out loud how I was going to make the drive alone. I pulled the phone away from my ear, looked in disbelief at the receiver, then reminded myself my father hadn't been around much when I was growing up and maybe that's why he didn't think of me as an adult.

I look over at David as he navigates through the El Paso streets. I was surprised when he said he'd come with me. I imagined him staying home, working his regular thirteen or fourteen hours a day on his projects. But yesterday he called from his office, told me he'd rearranged his appointments so he could drive me to El Paso.

I was happy I wouldn't have to make the trip alone. I've never told him or my father I don't like El Paso with its dirty air and the long drive up the snakelike highway to Dad's condo in Las Cruces.

"There it is," David says.

I look through the windshield, see the large sign: El Paso Hospital.

"Yeah, there it is."

David makes the turn then parks in the parking lot that spans two blocks. I climb out of the car and take a deep breath. The air is cold, dry, and I feel like a twig about to snap. I take my husband's hand as we walk through the double doors and begin looking for Dad's room. David's skin is warm, moist. We stay connected, and for a few soft moments I feel young and in love. When we find the room number Dad gave me, we break apart.

My father is propped up in bed. His tanned, muscled arms contrast the stark white sheet and blanket. He is staring out the window and doesn't hear us come in.

"Dad."

David walks to a chair in the farthest corner, places his hand on the back.

"Hi, Melinda." Dad's brown eyes are wide.

I cross the space between us and hug him as my heart pounds harder.

"I'm so sorry. I'm just so sorry." I begin to cry. He starts crying, too, his lips pulled into a shape I've never seen before.

"I'll stand right by you through this," I say, feel like I'm in a movie speaking words someone wrote.

"Hey, let's not get carried away around here," David booms from his chair. "This is curable, you know."

I turn, look at him. David's expression is one I don't recognize even though we've been together for twenty-two years. I pull away from my father. My husband has never been good with showing his emotions and this is just more proof.

"Hey, Dave, how's it going?" Dad says as if he wasn't crying a moment ago.

"Stan, how ya' doing?"

"Not so well. I guess you heard."

"Don't worry, they have lots of new methods for curing cancer."

I walk to the window across from the hospital bed and the two men slip easily to where they feel comfortable—talking about architecture and David's work. My father retired three years ago, but before,

everyone thought it funny I married an architect—
the same occupation as my dad.

They begin talking about David's latest contract
and my father's strong voice fills the room. I look out
the window. Below, at the back of the hospital, is a
small play area with swings, a little bit of grass. The
spring before my parents divorced, most evenings,
Dad and my mother took my sister Lena and me to
the small park by our house. We would run to the
swings, squealing, hop on. A moment later Dad
would stand next to us and instruct us on how to
pump our legs to make the swings go higher, then
he would explain velocity.

I was so afraid I would fall, but I gripped the metal
chains, pumped my legs hard because I wanted to
show him I could do better than Lena, swing perfectly. That spring I felt I could touch the cool spring
sky with my bare toes.

My mother always sat at a picnic table silently
watching us.

"Melinda?"

I glance over to Dad.

"Yes?"

"Would you mind picking up Jan from the airport?
I don't want her to take a cab."

"Jan's coming here?" I point to the floor and my father nods.

After my parents divorced, Dad married Jan, but then they divorced five years later. She's never wanted anything to do with my sister or me. I know this because when David and I moved to our new house in Grapevine, Dad stayed with us for two days on his way to Mexico. While I was unpacking dishes and David was at his office, I asked my father why we never spent a Christmas together after I turned sixteen. I was feeling brave, in the mood to fix our distant relationship.

There was a long silence, then he rubbed his face. "Jan never wanted me to have too much to do with you kids. I shouldn't have listened to her, but…" He got up from the couch and walked back to the guest room, closed the door.

I have never figured out what he was going to say. His life has always seemed so ideal. But that day I wanted him to tell me he was sorry. Before I had always thought my father didn't want to be close, he was a *loner*, as my mother had often said when she'd tried to explain him.

Silly as it sounds, his confession made his distance

from me easier to think about and validated why I never liked Jan.

"Jan's coming here?" I ask again, then smile, try to cover up my disappointment.

Three months after he and Jan were married, when I was sixteen, I visited my father for the last time. Jan backed me against the kitchen counter and explained in her breathy, Marilyn Monroe voice the many ways my father hated my mother. After, she put her index finger to her pursed lips and swore me to secrecy.

"Yeah, she thought I might have to have back surgery and she volunteered to take care of me while I was recovering. But that's all changed." He turns, stares out the door as if he's looking for someone. "So will you pick her up?"

"Of course I will."

I glance at my husband. We make eye contact and David raises his right eyebrow slightly. I turn away, tell myself the whole thing with Jan was a long time ago, she and my father are friends, and I need to get over any hard feelings.

"It would be easy for her to take a cab from the airport," David says.

I shake my head, try to signal to him to be quiet.

Like most husbands, there are times he drives me crazy.

My father's expression turns to worry and he pulls back the blanket a little.

"It's okay, Dad. I can pick her up." I glance at David, narrow my eyes. "I'd love to pick her up." And I wonder if all families play *nice* games, move tiny dry lies around so they don't have to talk about what they're really thinking.

"Thanks. I know she'll appreciate it." And then his gaze fills with something I've never seen before— maybe it's a mixture of appreciation and fear, but I just don't know my father well enough to be sure.

CHAPTER TWO

I watch Jan walk into the El Paso airport baggage area. She sees me, smiles, and I wave. I haven't seen her in years, but she looks the same—slim, pretty, but a little older. She's wearing a purple sweater and black stretch pants with a filmy lavender scarf draped around her shoulders.

"Hi," I say.

To my surprise, she wraps her arms around my shoulders, hugs me. She is smaller than I remember—for some reason I think of her as being bigger.

"How are you?" I ask.

She brushes at her sweater and her curly red hair falls forward a little. "This is what they're wearing in Seattle."

She has the same breathy Marilyn Monroe whisper. She looks up and studies me for a long moment. "How's Stanley?"

"He seems a little depressed, but I guess that's to

be expected. We have a meeting with the doctor tomorrow, so we'll get some answers then."

She nods, stares at me again.

I'm still stunned that my father is ill. When the nurse brought in all his pills this afternoon, I was amazed by the number. My father was always the one who insisted my sister and I eat whole-wheat bread when it wasn't popular, drink skim milk when no one else in the neighborhood drank the translucent liquid.

"I can't imagine my life without Stanley." Jan's voice sounds more childlike.

"A lot of people survive cancer. They have so many new treatments." I have the urge to tell her about my intuition—the dread I felt a few days ago but managed to push back. I'm determined to stay upbeat.

She looks at me, eyes wide. "That's all I'll let myself think about, too."

"Good." I pat her arm and we walk to the baggage carousel.

When we reach my car, I place Jan's huge suitcase in the trunk.

"It's so cold." She hugs herself. "I didn't think it would be this cold here."

"Did you bring a coat?"

She shakes her head.

"How long can you stay?"

"I'll stay as long as Stanley needs me."

"I brought an extra coat. You can borrow it, if you want. Or we can go buy you one tomorrow."

"Thanks. That's nice of you."

We climb in the car. I turn on the heater and soon we are out of the parking lot and on the highway to the hospital. I look over and she smiles at me then runs her fingers through her hair.

"Stanley and I were going to take a driving trip to Colorado after he got better from his back surgery." She sighs. "You know how he loves to travel."

"I bet you still will be able to. This afternoon, at the hospital, he told me about that trip."

"I just can't believe Stanley has cancer." She shakes her head and her feathery voice fills the car.

"It's nice you came to help my father."

She touches my shoulder. "I'm sorry about Stanley."

My muscles relax a little. "I know, so am I. It just seems weird that Dad's sick. He's never sick."

"It's going to be okay." Her eyes narrow a little and she pats my right arm again then stares straight ahead.

She still has a pretty profile. When I first met her, she told me she loved being an Earl Carroll showgirl in Hollywood. I smile at the memory. When I was young, I was fascinated that Jan was a dancer. After my parents' divorce, my mother and I fought a lot, sometimes bitterly. I was probably looking for a friend, and I wanted so much for Jan to like me.

Maybe now we can get to know each other a little better.

"How are Bob and Verna?" she asks halfway to the hospital.

"Fine. They brought Dad to El Paso the other day." Three years ago, when Dad retired, he planned to move to Seattle. He and Jan were going to try to live together again, but they had a major blowup, over what I don't know. Then, suddenly, Dad moved to Las Cruces where his friends the Skillys live.

I park in the hospital parking lot and we go inside. David is sitting in the same chair where I left him, reading a *Time* magazine, and Dad is staring out the window.

"Hey, look who's here." I smile, make an effort to sound and look happy.

Dad turns, sees Jan and his expression softens.

"Hey, honey, how are you?" Dad's voice is not as tense as it was before I left for the airport.

Jan starts to cross the space between them, but in the middle of the room she stops, begins to sob and covers her face with her hands.

"Oh, Stanley! I can't believe this is happening." Jan manages to go to my father and hug him.

I look at David. This is just the kind of behavior that makes him uncomfortable. He rolls his eyes.

A moment later a nurse walks in with a tray. "Mr. Howard, here's your dinner."

Jan, now sitting on the edge of the hospital bed, straightens, looks at her. Her face is streaked with tears and smeared black mascara rims her eyes.

"Hello," she says. Her normal voice is deep and reminds me of a cartoon cat. We reshuffle, Jan in a chair by the bed, holding my father's hand, David and I sitting across from them. After the nurse leaves, we dive into conversation about Jan's flight as if it's a heated swimming pool.

My father doesn't eat, only takes two sips of water. Jan begins eating large forkfuls of chicken and mashed potatoes. Suddenly my husband shakes his head and I know he's going to say something I won't like.

"Don't you think Stan should be eating that?" he asks Jan.

She stares at him, still chewing, spoon midair. "Well, I—I'm hungry."

"There's a cafeteria downstairs."

I laugh nervously, give everyone my *let's play nice* smile. My father's ex-wife is here to take care of him. And I want to think about other things besides illness and making an ex-stepmother happy.

David and I are standing by Dad's hospital bed, listening to Dr. Garces talk about my father's condition. The doctor is younger than I imagined he would be. Jan isn't here. When she heard we were meeting with Dad's doctor, she decided to go to the gift shop to buy her grandson a present.

"Your father's cancer has metastasized from his prostate and settled in his spine," Dr. Garces says in a quiet voice. "I'm going to refer him to an oncologist in Las Cruces."

David and I nod and Dad stares straight ahead, doesn't move. I have questions that have been roaming around my mind for days—like how long it will be before my father gets better—but I can't make the questions come out of my mouth. I guess

I'm afraid if I ask a question and there's a negative answer, the desperate look on my father's face will deepen.

"What's really important is we keep a positive attitude," Dr. Garces says.

"I think so, too. I read somewhere that a positive outlook can really help any illness," I say, then smile.

"No one can predict how the cancer will progress. If a patient and his family are positive, it has a better effect on everyone."

I focus on my father. He looks as if someone has just turned a garden hose on him. I'm on the verge of crying, but I shake the feeling away. My tears won't help him and that's all I want to do.

"I think that's right," I say instead.

"If you have any questions, call me, anytime." Dr. Garces shakes my father's hand, then ours and walks out of the room.

David and I sit in our chairs. I expected the doctor to tell us my father's cancer is very curable and he should have no problems recovering, that in a few months his life will be back to almost normal. But all he really told us was that Dad would be seeing another doctor and to keep a positive attitude.

Jan walks into the room, hugging a large, fuzzy, brown teddy bear. She stops in the middle of the room, glances from face to face, and her expression crumbles. She puts the teddy bear on the bed at my father's feet and sits in the chair closest to him.

"Stanley, are you okay?"

"Yeah, I'm fine."

David gets up, walks into the hallway, and I follow him to give my father and Jan some time alone. My husband leans against the wall, folds his arms.

"We probably should go home tomorrow." His tone is flat, dry.

"What?"

He stares at the floor and then looks at me. "I've got work waiting for me at the office. Besides, there's not a lot we can do here."

My heart begins to pound and my mouth feels dry. I know he has things to do at work, and this isn't his responsibility, but it's so nice to have my husband here while I try to help my father.

"I'd like you to stay. I know it's not a lot of fun, but I want to be here for a few more days to make sure Dad's okay."

David shakes his head. "You should come home,

too. Your father will be okay with Jan here." He nods back toward the hospital room. "The doctor said he's going to release him tomorrow."

"Maybe I can make Dad look at his condition more positively. He seems a little depressed. I mean, I would be, too, but maybe I could help him see that his attitude is going to affect his recovery time." I stop, look down the hall and then back to David, hoping he's smiling, but he isn't.

"I wish Dad would have asked the doctor some questions." I gesture to the room.

"Maybe he doesn't want to know the answers." David stands straighter, uncrosses his arms. "It's got to be tough for him."

At least this is something we both agree on.

David and I are at our neighbor Elizabeth's house. She and her husband Brad invited us over for dinner. We came home from Las Cruces three days ago, the day my father was released from the hospital. I never managed to cheer up my father, and I've been worried about him since we left.

Yesterday Elizabeth called and I gladly accepted her invitation to dinner. I want to be with friends, laugh and not worry for a few hours. Elizabeth invited another couple, Jim and Deanne Smith. The six of us have spent many evenings together, like this one, enjoying drinks, eating dinner, talking about the neighborhood. Sometimes Deanne and I talk about our children. Elizabeth and Brad don't have children, yet she seems happy to hear about my Jenny and Deanne's two.

Right now, our husbands are standing at Brad's bar, a throwback from his bachelor days. They are laughing about something. David is behind the bar, and I'm happy he is having a good time.

Deanne, Elizabeth and I are sitting on stools at the kitchen counter. Stuffed manicotti bakes in the oven and everyone is drinking Sapphire gin and tonics. If someone were to look through the kitchen window right now, they would see a perfect evening.

Elizabeth touches my hand and I turn toward her.

"I'm glad you and David came over." She takes a sip of her drink and I watch the lime slice bob between the ice cubes.

"Yeah, it's good we can all get together," Deanne says.

I don't feel as close to Deanne. At times, she's distant, almost cold, the opposite of Elizabeth. I felt an instant connection with Elizabeth when we met eight years ago at one of David's work-related dinners. Elizabeth is a hospice nurse and Brad has worked with David for years.

"I'm glad we're here, too. After the last few days, I need some laughs." I glance over at David again. He's listening intently to Jim. He looks nice in his long-sleeved white shirt and khakis. I catch his eye, lift my glass and he does the same.

"How's your father?" Deanne asks. She studies her left hand and picks at the cuticle of her ring finger.

Elizabeth takes my hand and squeezes it for a moment. "Yeah, how's he doing?"

"Dad's doing great," I say, although this isn't true.

Deanne looks up. "What did the doctors say?"

"That Dad needs to keep a positive attitude. The cancer came from his prostate. You know, he's never been sick a day in his life. But he'll be okay. He's so strong." I force myself to smile. I feel like I'm about to cry, but I don't want to do that here.

How can I explain that the doctor never really gave us any real information except that we need to stay positive? And since David and I came home, my father won't come to the phone when I call?

"That's understandable," Elizabeth says in her

calm voice. "You know, if you wanted, you could bring him here, and I could help you take care of him."

I study her. She's so kind, thoughtful, but I can't imagine my father coming here or me taking care of him. We don't have a relationship like that. He's so independent and we've never really spent a lot of time together. Besides, in a few months he'll be better.

"I don't think he'd come here. Plus he has to take six radiation treatments."

"When he gets worse, it'll be difficult to bring him here," Elizabeth says.

When he gets worse! For a moment, the words make my chest hurt and my throat burn. I swallow, breathe in. I've heard a lot of stories about people beating cancer, and if anyone can do it, my dad will.

"I think he's going to get better," I say.

"Prostate cancer can be unpredictable when it's in the bone. I've dealt with a lot of patients like your father," Elizabeth says.

"And I've heard of lots of people surviving. My father's a strong man."

"Yes, some do."

"Dad's that kind of person. In a year they'll

probably write about him in the *Journal of the American Medical Association*." My father used to run for miles, train for marathons and still work long hours.

The guys laugh, the three of us look over at them, and I'm grateful for the diversion.

"Listen to them," Deanne says. "They're sure having a good time. What do you suppose they're talking about?"

"Let's see, either sports or work, or both. Certainly not us," Elizabeth says.

There won't be any need for my father to come here. In a few months, he'll be taking a trip with Jan, laughing, feeling relieved that he beat cancer.

"I'm sure my father's going to get better." The words fall from my lips before I can stop them.

The two women turn to me and Elizabeth's eyes narrow a little.

"He's always been so strong, a runner…anything he put his mind to he did." I gesture toward where I think Las Cruces might be from Elizabeth's kitchen.

Deanne nods. "I'm sure he will."

"Everyone is different," Elizabeth says.

"My goal is to cheer him up. I call him every

day." I leave out the fact that Jan has told me he won't talk to anyone.

Over at the bar, David is looking at me. Did he hear what I just said? He lifts his gin and tonic. I raise my glass again then take a long sip. An ice cube touches my tongue, feels so cold.

I place the chilly glass back on the napkin, right in the middle and press the lifted corner with my fingertip.

"I don't understand men. They just don't want to be sick or inconvenienced," Deanne says. "When I told Jim about your father, he asked me if we could talk about something else. They certainly don't want to think about illness. When I was in labor with Ellie, he couldn't stand it."

I imagine my father lying in his bed. I push the image out of my mind. Elizabeth's kitchen clock says six-thirty. I wonder what Jan and Dad are doing right now? Maybe they're watching TV, sitting on the couch, laughing.

"…and then, when I came home from the hospital, Jim didn't even want to hear about my sore nipples."

Elizabeth laughs. I laugh, too, pretend I was listening.

"Well, I wouldn't want to hear about them, either." Elizabeth gets off the bar stool, goes to the oven and opens the door.

I sniff. The gin has kicked in and I feel more relaxed, the alcohol buffing some of my edginess. The manicotti smells delicious, rich, comforting, and for the first time in days I'm actually hungry.

I am standing in the breakfast nook of our brick home, looking out at the front yard. The morning is flooded with pink sunrise and the bare tree branches make an interesting pattern against the opal-like sky. The purple pansies David planted weeks ago ring the ground around the tree trunk. The bright flowers are doing fine, even though it's been cold. Beneath the pansies, deep in the earth, are the rough daffodil bulbs I planted months ago.

This morning, right before David left, he announced he'd be home late. I stood in the garage, next to the door to the house and smiled, told him not to worry, I have plenty to do. Then I explained that I was going to clean house, straighten some drawers, rearrange the hall closet and then maybe go to the library and help out. He waved like he always does and climbed into his Avalon.

I sit at the breakfast table, take a sip of my coffee.
I love our home in the mornings. Watching the
sunrise from our breakfast nook always gives me an
awesome feeling. At times, when I'm really busy, I
forget about nature's beauty until I sit here and
watch the world turn pink and gold.

My favorite coffee mug is warming my hands.
Jenny gave it to me for Easter eleven years ago, when
she was nine. She was such a cute and serious little
girl. That year, she made David drive her to the drugstore, and she came back with this oversize white
mug filled with blue jellybeans. On the outside of the
mug is a picture of a cartoon rabbit catching jellybeans
in an upside-down umbrella. The rabbit is drawn in
thin circles and there's a tiny raised blue jellybean for
his nose. That beautiful afternoon, she and I sat at this
table in our old house and ate all the candy.

After, we laughed, and I could see that her mouth
had turned blue. I told her about it, and we both got
up and looked in the mirror. Mine was blue, too.
Now she's a serious college student at the University of Texas, majoring in pharmacy. I miss the
bubbling of a child in the house, going to PTA
meetings, listening to gossip about her friends.

I turn a little and the neat stack of papers I

brought home from the hospital—information about cancer and treatments—catches my eye. I should read all of it, learn about my father's disease, but there is something deep inside me that doesn't want to know any more than I already do.

More sunshine breaks through—yellow-white—eating up the opal-like sky. I get up, take my mug into the kitchen, stand at the sink and pour out my coffee. I need to keep busy, vacuum, dust, scrub bathrooms. The last year I taught junior high I began feeling restless. I told David and he suggested I quit because financially we were doing fine. But I didn't want to break my teaching contract, so I trudged through each day, telling myself the school year would end soon.

I quit June first, the same day the kids climbed on the buses for the last time. The moment I walked out of the principal's office, I felt better. I'm not sure I want to go back to teaching, but I don't know what else I could do. And for the past seven months I've enjoyed staying home, cleaning out closets, keeping the house in perfect order.

David says it's fine, that I've worked for years and I should take a break or retire early, but in a lot of ways I miss working—the friendships, the creativity of teaching.

The phone rings and the sound startles me a little. It's probably David, letting me know what time he'll be home for dinner. I pick it up and hear Jan's whisper.

"I can't understand you," I say. "What's the matter?" I'm in the breakfast nook again, looking out the window, my heart pounding.

She says more breathy words I can't decipher.

"Is Dad okay? Jan, you have to speak up."

"The garage door is broken and the water heater went out last night," she says in her normal voice—the cartoon cat one.

I take a breath, relax a little. Dad's household problems can be fixed. "Did you call a repairman?"

"Stanley is so depressed. He won't eat, won't get out of bed. I don't know what to do."

"Why won't he eat?" I've never known my father not to eat, not take care of himself.

"I don't know. And he said he's not going to do any more radiation treatments."

My heart races more. He's had half the treatments, Jan driving him to the radiation clinic a few miles from his condo.

"Let me talk to him." But I know he won't come to the phone. I've called twice a day since we came home and have only spoken with Jan.

"He's so depressed, he doesn't want to talk to anyone."

"What can I do?" I begin to feel a little sick to my stomach.

"Come here. He seemed okay when you were here."

I was hoping my father and Jan would get into a routine, Dad going to his radiation treatments, Jan taking care of him. At night when the house is quiet, I imagine Dad getting better, and later, talking about how awful this time was. Yet, deep down, I knew when I left Las Cruces, it wasn't going to play out that way.

"He wants me there?"

"Yes, he wasn't so depressed when you were here."

"Okay, I'll talk to David and call you back," I say then hang up. Although my father is ill, I'm happy he wants my company, that I can help him in some way.

I look out to the yard and wish things were the way they were the day I planted the daffodils. My life was so calm, so perfect that early October afternoon.

CHAPTER THREE

David and I are standing in the garage by his workbench. After I hung up with Jan, I called him and explained that I need to go back to New Mexico. He didn't say much except we'd talk when he got home.

I cleaned house all morning to keep busy then packed and repacked my suitcase. I kept changing my mind on what I should take, folding different jeans, T-shirts and sweaters then hanging them back up. After I finally got packed, I spent three hours in the kitchen, making dinner—Paprika Chicken, David's favorite and chicken stew. When I heard the garage door open, I rushed through the house to meet him.

The garage door is still open and a crisp winter wind blows brown leaves under our cars.

"Why do you have to go back there so soon?" he asks.

"I told you, Dad's condo has some problems, and Jan said he's depressed. Maybe I can cheer him up." I stop, realize I'm breathless. "She said he feels better when I am there."

David rubs his left eye with the back of his hand. He looks tired, and I feel awful for not even letting him come into the house before I started telling him about this.

"I'd be depressed, too, if I had an ex-wife taking care of me. Hasn't that woman ever heard of a repairman? If she can't handle the house, how is she going to help your father?"

"I had a feeling Jan taking care of Dad wasn't going to be that easy. She says he won't eat, doesn't want any more radiation treatments. Maybe they need some moral support." I shrug. "What else can I do?"

"She couldn't leave you alone for a few more days? We just got back. I don't think it's a good idea to run there every time she calls. What did Stan say?"

"He won't come to the phone." I hug myself. "You'd do the same for your mother." This isn't true. David would send money, call—but he wouldn't worry like I have. Most men are different that way, and maybe they're better off.

"No, my sister would do it. And what about *your* sister?"

I laugh, shake my head at his question. David knows how my sister Lena is. She won't fly, won't take car trips. She's a barrel of anxieties, lives on disability and borrows money from Dad. She still tries to get money from me, and I used to lend it to her until I realized she was never going to pay us back.

"You know how my sister is."

"Yeah."

Whenever I bad-mouth my sister to my father, he always explains what a hard beginning Lena had, before my parents adopted her. My mother was told she might not be able to get pregnant and she wanted a child desperately. They adopted Lena when she was six months old. She only weighed nine pounds. Her fourteen-year-old mother had left her with relatives who'd neglected her.

Every time Dad tells me she had a rough beginning, I know he's right, until the next time Lena tries to hit me up for five hundred dollars. And even though she's four years older than I am, most of my life I have felt like the older sister.

"So how long do you think you'll stay?" David

moves a screwdriver with a yellow handle from one side of his workbench to the other.

"Not long. I'll just get the condo straightened out, cheer Dad up, come back as soon as I can. I figure three days will be enough to get the repairs done."

"When do you want to leave?"

"I got an airline ticket for tomorrow. I was looking online and it was such a good deal, I was afraid I'd lose it. You could come with me if you want to. Dad was better when you were there."

"I've got too many projects. Besides, with Jan there, your father's condo is too crowded. I'll hold the fort down here."

He walks to the remote button, hits it hard and the garage door rumbles shut.

We are in bed. I have the TV on, and David is lying on his back waiting for me to turn off the TV so he can go to sleep. The gray-and-white light from "Leave It to Beaver" illuminates our bedroom. June is talking to Ward in their spotless kitchen, but I have the set on mute so I have no idea what problem they're solving.

"Isn't it wonderful I got a good deal on an airline ticket," I say, although this isn't true.

"What airline again?" He yawns and so do I.

"American."

"How much?"

I close my eyes, continue to shade the truth. "One ninety-eight." The ticket actually cost almost three hundred dollars. I put it on a credit card I have that David doesn't know about—one I got when I was teaching. I don't like doing this, but sometimes I don't tell the truth about money just to avoid a fight. David has always worried about our finances. I'm sure it's because his father died when he was eight and their family struggled financially after that. He's explained how they never had enough and he wouldn't have been able to go to college if he hadn't gotten an academic scholarship. I guess our childhoods follow us around whether we want them to or not.

"That price isn't bad," he says.

I relax a little, wet my lips. "While I'm gone you'll have plenty to eat. There's the leftover Paprika Chicken, and the stew I made this afternoon." I felt good as I neatly stacked food in the fridge—knew David would have home-cooked meals until I come home.

But now guilt slides up my spine, hitting each

vertebra. I'm spending too much money and then lying about it, leaving my husband to fend for himself, and I'm sure the food won't last for long.

"Great." He turns to me, reaches out and musses my hair. "We'd better go to sleep. We both have long days in front of us."

I turn off the TV, lean over, kiss his cheek. His skin is warm.

When David begins to snore softly, I quietly get out of bed and walk through the house. Icy winter moonlight illuminates each room and the tile floor feels cold against my feet. In the breakfast nook, I look out to the yard and the oak tree. The full moon is dousing the earth with cold glassy light. The tree branches, the grass and pansies are the same color as June and Ward.

I'm sitting on the edge of my father's king-size bed, holding a large glass of water. He has been in here most of the day. A little while ago in the kitchen I put a red plastic straw in the glass, hoping he would drink more water.

Dad's eyes are closed, but I know he's not asleep. Gina, his home health care nurse, who left thirty minutes ago, told me he's dehydrated and needs to drink water. So for the last thirty minutes I've been urging him to take sips of water. He did drink some, but a moment ago he said he'd had enough.

This morning I drove him to the radiation clinic. After I got to Las Cruces, I convinced him to continue with the treatments. All I did was sit next to him on the couch, tell him I thought it would be best that he go back to the radiation center. He nodded his head, said he would. Then I explained I thought everything was going to be okay. A moment later he got up and went back to bed.

When Dad and I got to the clinic this morning, we sat quietly in the waiting room. I leafed through old *Southern Living* magazines, and my father stared at the carpet. I looked over at him, realized he's lost a lot of weight.

I've been in Las Cruces for four days. David told me this morning that he ran out of the food last night, and tonight he'll stop by JR's for dinner.

"Dad," I say, resettle myself on the edge of the bed because my back is beginning to ache from no support.

He looks at me.

"Have a little more water."

"No." He shuts his eyes again.

I stare at the three Frank Lloyd Wright awards on

the wall. My father has won many awards for building designs, but these are the most prestigious, proof that he has an ironclad will for doing everything flawlessly.

"Dad, the nurse says you need to drink more water. You're dehydrated. Just take a few sips, then I'll leave you alone." It feels so strange telling my father what to do.

"'Water, water, everywhere, nor any drop to drink.'" His voice is raspy, as if he's thirsty, yet he enunciates each word perfectly.

I laugh. He used to quote this poem when I was a kid and we were traveling. Lena and I, from the back seat of the car, would beg him to stop at a Quick-Stop so we could get Cokes. When he refused, Lena would tell him we were dying of thirst. He'd look at us through rearview mirror, recite that line.

He opens his eyes. "Melinda, I don't want any more water. I've had enough."

"Are you sure?"

He nods once.

"If you're hungry I'll fix you something to eat."

"No. I'm fine."

"Do you want to talk?"

"I'm too tired."

He closes his eyes again and I study his face. His skin is smooth and he doesn't look seventy-two. After he retired, I called him every two weeks, worried that since he'd been such a workaholic, he might not adapt to retirement. But he got along just fine and was busy as ever with traveling, his volunteer work, his friends, Jan. On the phone we'd discuss politics, his trips or teaching, nothing personal, but it was nice to talk to him.

"Okay," I say.

He looks at me. "Okay?"

"I can't make you drink more water. I do remember that poem, though. Lena would claim she was so thirsty she was dying, and you wouldn't stop the car because we were on a tight schedule."

"Yeah, I was always in a hurry."

"Oh, we survived. Do you remember the rest of the poem?"

"I do."

"Remember, sometimes Mom interrupted, finished a line for you."

He sits up a little, pushes back against the pillow but doesn't say anything.

"Mom gave me the book of poetry you and she used to read from, when you were both in college."

He turns his head a little. "Oh, really?"

"It was years ago, when I was going to school. She said I might be able to use it." I place the water glass on the nightstand and watch the straw circle to the other side. "There are margin notes by some of the poems."

"She and I used to go to the park, read poetry out loud."

"'Water, water, everywhere, nor any drop to drink.' I always liked that even though you wouldn't stop for Cokes."

He shakes his head. "Back then there never seemed to be enough time. Now there's too much."

Another memory surfaces—Lena and I in the back seat, my parents in the front, my mother sitting close to him, and he has his arm around her.

"I forget. Who's the poem by?"

Dad closes his eyes, licks his lips. They look dry and chapped. I need to get him some Chap Stick at the store tomorrow.

"Coleridge. It's the '*Rime of the Ancient Mariner*.'"

"I used to love when you'd recite it."

"'God save thee, ancient Mariner!'" He smiles at me and I smile back.

"Did Mom memorize some of it, too?"

MARY SCHRAMSKI   53

"I don't know. I had to memorize it to win a contest in school. First prize was ten dollars. Back then ten dollars was like a million. We didn't have much money. It took me three months."

"You memorized the entire poem?"

He nods and I imagine my father as boy, trying to put each line to memory. I'm not surprised though. He's always been determined.

"Yeah, I was the only one in the school who could recite it perfectly."

"What did you buy with the money?"

"I gave it to my mother for food." He closes his eyes again. "I'm so tired."

I pat his shoulder, get up and walk through the living room into the kitchen. Three mugs half full of cold tea sit next to the sink. Dried-out tea bags, like winter leaves on our front porch in Texas, dot the counter, stain the white Formica. Jan loves tea and makes cup after cup, leaving a trail of tea bags behind her like Hansel and Gretel.

I look through the pass-through above the sink. She is sitting on the couch, the phone pressed between her right shoulder and ear. I hear her laugh, say, *Oh, Donny,* and I know she's talking to her only child. Before Dad, Jan was married to a colonel in the air force and they had Donny. He's thirty-three, a problem man-child who's been in jail three times for drunk driving.

"Things are the same. Oh, Stanley's daughter, Melinda, is here."

Jan looks back to me, holds up her mug and smiles deeply. I have learned this means she would like another cup of tea. I turn to the stove, grab the kettle, fill it with water, place it on the burner, snap the control to high and hear the familiar hiss—fire licking metal.

"We're bonding, Donny. She's nice. You'd really like her."

Jan's words remind me I have not seen my ex-stepbrother in a long time. I try to think of the last time but only know it was when he was a child.

"It's a lot of work for me, but I have to do it for Stanley. Work, work, work, there's nothing else," she says in her breathy persona as she flips her hand back and forth.

Jan has her back to me now, and I wonder if she knows I can hear her.

Work, work, work, my foot! Since I've been here, she sleeps till ten, sits on the couch and goes to lunch with Verna and Bob Skilly. I have encouraged her to do these things because I know it must be difficult for her to see my father depressed and in bed most of the time. And I appreciate that she has come to help him.

But in the last four days, I've cleaned the condo, arranged for the garage and water heater repairs, driven my father to his appointments, tried to get him to eat and drink and listened to her complain about how inept he was as a husband.

I have swallowed back the hurt that rises in my throat when she talks about him. I haven't said anything to her about this because I don't want to cause a problem.

The teakettle whistles, I fill her mug, dunk the tea bag up and down until the water is dark. I add two teaspoons of sugar, get the milk from the fridge. The carton's opening is smeared with her red lipstick. I pour milk in the tea, put the carton back in the refrigerator.

Yesterday morning I was going to have cereal, but when I found the carton in such shape, I put it back, pictured Jan, late at night, lit in the glaring refrigerator light, head tipped back, guzzling milk. Instead I poured orange juice over my Raisin Bran, hoping she didn't drink that from that carton, too.

I walk out to the living room, hand her the tea. She smiles and so do I. I know she is trying to be nice. I make it across the living room, to the edge of the dining room where I've folded my blanket and stacked pillows—the place where I sleep because Jan is in the guest room. She also told me when I first got here that she needs the couch late at night when she can't sleep.

"Okay, baby, I'll call you tomorrow." She hangs up, sighs. "Melinda."

I turn back reluctantly, want to like her, but there are so many things about her that drive me crazy.

"I've probably talked to him more this week than I have in months."

I want to say, *And all on my father's dime*, but I don't. I feel bad for even thinking it. She has come here to take care of my father, and I should be thankful for that. I only wish she would actually do a little work while she's here.

I nod, press my mean thoughts and words back where I hope they stay. "It's nice you can talk to him."

"He remembers you. He's had his problems, but he's straightened out."

I think, *It's about time*, close my eyes against the words, then I smile at her again.

"That's good, Jan." I walk into the kitchen, begin

cleaning up. Through the pass-through, I see her get off the couch, cross the living room and head toward the kitchen. She sits at the pine table that holds the computer my father bought three months ago but has not used.

I sweep tea bags and crushed napkins into the trash, run water for the dishes. I really don't feel like cleaning, but it will keep me from having to shift my full attention to her.

"Before Stanley and I were married, he was so nice to Donny." Her voice is thin, baby-like.

I know she's gearing up for one of her negative stories about my father. I wash a mug and watch a tea bag float in between the soap bubbles.

"The first year we were dating, Stanley fixed Donny's bicycle, took him places, but then after we got married…it was like Donny didn't exist. When Stanley moved down here and volunteered at the grammar school, well, I thought that is the *perfect* place for Stanley. He can help then walk away with no commitment."

The anger I've tamped down turns over, groans, but I press it back. Maybe if I don't say anything she'll stop or talk about how she misses Seattle. *That* I can relate to. Right now I'd like to be sitting in my sunrise-filled breakfast nook, drinking from the coffee mug Jenny gave me.

"I never understood why he volunteered at the grammar school. He never liked kids."

"I suggested he volunteer," I say, remembering when he called me from Las Cruces right after he moved here and told me how lonely he was. I told him to call a senior volunteer program. He did and for a year he was a first-grade teacher's aide at a school filled with Hispanic children. I was happy for him because he was getting a kick out of the kids and making friends with other volunteers.

"Like I said, I thought it was strange, but then I realized it was perfect for him because he didn't have to make a commitment or really get involved. That's how he likes it—his life without any ties."

"Don't we all. But he took some great pictures of the kids." I submerge my hands in the hot water, remember the black-and-white photos he showed me of the happy young faces staring up into his camera lens. He snapped the photos right before Easter. They were perfect—artistic, beautiful.

"Some of those kids never had their pictures taken till Dad took them." I manage to keep the edge out of my voice.

"Well, you know Stanley. He's not much of a kid person. He's never come to see Donny's son."

"Weren't you two divorced by then?" This slips out as I stare at the dishwater. Oh, God, why can't I just keep my mouth shut? She's so sensitive about their divorce and my father not moving to Seattle.

"Well…" There's a tiny bit of shock in her voice, and this makes me feel better for a moment before I realize my remark was small and petty.

"But we were always good friends, even after our divorce. Oh, I don't know what I'll do without him if this doesn't come out okay."

I wash the last mug, turn around, know I have to get out of the kitchen before I say something else I'll be sorry for. Plus I need space, some air. "Are you finished?"

"Not quite. I'm nursing it a little." She takes a small sip of her tea, looks at me over the rim. "You know your father and I had a great sex life."

Oh, my God.

I face the sink, mop the clean counter with the sponge. *This* I do not need to hear.

"He's a great lover. I never liked it with any other man, but with Stanley, well, that's a different story—"

"Dishes are finally done! Tea bags are where they should be, in the trash," I say over her whisper. "I'm going to the store."

CHAPTER FOUR

I'm standing in the doorway of Dad's bedroom trying to convince him he should eat dinner. His condo smells of baked chicken, like our home in Grapevine does on winter evenings when it's cold outside and the windows gleam yellow against the darkness.

Homesickness fills my chest and eyes, but I push it back, focus on my father.

"Dad, you should eat," I say again, try to sound happy. I'm stuck between trying not to be too pushy and wanting the best for him.

His condo is quiet tonight. An hour ago, Jan drove over to the Skillys' for dinner. She asked Dad to go with her, but he shook his head, said he was too tired. This morning, I called his doctor's office and explained my father is always tired. The nurse told me the exhaustion could be the effects from the radiation. Dad now has an appointment for next week.

Before Jan left, she asked if I minded if she went to the Skillys for dinner. *Did I mind?* I laughed and told her I was happy she could get out, and I am. But I'm also enjoying the quiet. Jan follows me around the condo and talks nonstop. I know talking helps her relax, feel calmer, but it drives me crazy, so crazy I now look forward to taking my father for his radiation treatment just to get away from her.

Dad turns over.

"Do you want to eat some dinner?" I ask. "I made chicken, mashed potatoes, spinach."

He sits up a little, gives me a half smile. "That was nice of you, honey, but I'm not hungry."

I walk into the room, stand by his bed.

"Dad, do you think you're depressed?"

"I don't know what I am."

"Your home health nurse said it's important you eat. I don't want to nag, but could you eat just a little?"

"Did Jan leave?"

"About an hour ago." I cross my arms. "Is she being okay? I mean, is she being nice to you?"

"Yeah, she's fine." He sits up more, swings his legs to the floor. His gray hair is matted in places, sticking out in others. He doesn't look like himself.

MARY SCHRAMSKI   63

"Okay, I'll eat, just something small. If you will," he says.

My heart pounds with happiness. "I'll go fix our plates."

In the kitchen, I take the chicken out of the oven. Dad has the minimum cooking utensils, so putting dinner together was interesting. I baked the chicken in a frying pan, and the mashed potatoes are a little lumpy because I had to mash them with a fork. Before, Dad ate at Luby's Cafeteria almost every night. While I was cooking tonight, I realized how one can make do, substitute one thing for another.

My father walks into the living room and sits on the couch, smoothes his wrinkled pajamas legs.

"Dad," I say through the kitchen pass-through.

He glances back to where I am.

"You want chicken, mashed potatoes *and* spinach?"

"I don't know." He sighs, turns back around and my spirits fall.

I stare at the back of his head, his hair so messy, and wonder what I should do. A memory surfaces, when I was eleven. My mother said the back of my father's head looked like Cary Grant's.

"Your father has a wonderfully shaped head," she

said from across the dining table. It was the year before they divorced. "Just like Cary Grant's."

"Who's he?" I asked.

My mother looked at me in wonder, as if she couldn't believe her eleven-year-old daughter didn't know who Cary Grant was.

"Melinda, Cary Grant is the most handsome movie star in the world. And he has a perfectly shaped head." Her beautiful white hands, nails painted ginger-pink, pressed against the warm wood.

"Stanley, did you hear me? You have the most beautifully shaped head."

My father was in the living room putting on a Mantovani record, and it felt nice they weren't arguing, seemed so happy.

"What?" he yelled.

"The back of your head is shaped just like Cary Grant's."

He walked back into the dining room laughing. "I know, Hanna. You always say that when you've had a glass of wine. My head does not look like Cary Grant's."

"Oh, you're so hardheaded."

They laughed at the same time. And Lena and I looked at each other, began laughing, too. My father kept smiling, went around the table, stood in front of my mother and took her hand, stroked her arm.

"You know, Hanna, I'm easy to get along with. You said so the other night."

"I never said that."

He drew an invisible circle on the back of her hand and she giggled like a girl.

"Oh, yes, you did."

She smiled deeply, stood up and began singing "Some Enchanted Evening" along with the music playing in the living room.

I sat very still, held my breath.

"Dad, dance with her," Lena yelled, stood and then immediately sat in her chair.

I couldn't utter a word because I was too busy staring at how beautiful they looked together—my mother in her yellow Easter dress, my father in a crisp white shirt and dark green slacks.

"Okay, I'll dance with your mother." He pulled her to him and they glided around the dining table three times.

Dad coughs, brings me back to the condo kitchen.

"Dad, you need to eat something." I stare at the back of his head, the memory of our family that happy Easter still washing through me.

"Okay, I will."

"Really?"

"Yes. But not a lot."

I pick up the empty plate that has been waiting patiently for my father and place a slice of chicken, two tablespoons of spinach and a small, irregular circle of mashed potatoes on the plate. I feel a little like I'm encouraging a bird. Steam curls up around my fingers from the small hill of food.

A moment later I'm standing in front of him with my offering. He takes it. The house has a church-like silence without Jan, and I breath in its blessings—my father eating, the quiet.

"Would you rather eat at the table?" I ask.

"I'm fine here. Get something for yourself, honey. There's some wine in the cabinet."

I want to say, *Oh, I've found the wine,* but I nod instead, hope if I eat he'll eat more. I go back to the kitchen, plop mashed potatoes on my plate, spear some chicken. I think about the bottle of wine, but I'm afraid to have another glass because my emotions are as fragile as glass.

I go back to the living room and sit next to Dad on the couch.

"This looks really good if I say so myself." I fork

potatoes into my mouth. My father takes a bite of spinach and my heart fills with hope. Spinach is filled with vitamins, antioxidants. It has to be good for fighting cancer.

We are quiet as we eat. I wolf down my plate of food, nod as I'm eating, hope to show him how good it is.

My father eats slowly, chewing with determination.

"I guess I was hungrier than I thought." I put my empty plate on the coffee table, look at him, smile.

"You've worked hard. You should be hungry." He forks a dab of potatoes into his mouth, swallows and sighs.

"Oh, not that hard." I lie. "I had fun making dinner. Working in your kitchen is a real challenge."

"You know, I've never been sick a day in my life… till now."

I rack my brain trying to think of something I can say to encourage him, make him less depressed, yet I feel like I'm talking to someone I barely know.

"Remember when Lena and I were kids, you were the healthiest parent on the block? Every father wanted to be like you. Didn't you have weights in the garage you used to lift?"

Dad nods, his lips thin. "Yeah, after dinner. I'd go out there. That seems like a long time ago."

"I was just thinking about an Easter you and Mom danced around the dining room. She always said the back of your head looked like Cary Grant's."

"Your mother was quite the exaggerator." He chuckles and my body relaxes more. Funny how, in just a few weeks, the road to happiness can change direction, be resurfaced with consumed food, a father's joke.

"Yeah, I was always so healthy. If I ever get out of this mess…I'll…"

"You'll what, Dad? Do you want to travel more?" He shakes his head.

"What do you want to do?"

"You notice they aren't giving me chemo. Most cancer patients get chemo, not just radiation. I've been wondering about that."

"Maybe you should ask the doctor."

"Maybe I don't want to know."

"The doctor said every case is different." But the tiny bit of dread in the pit of my stomach rolls over, reminds me it's there. "I'll ask your doctor if you want me to."

"No." He places his plate on the coffee table,

leans back and grips his thighs as if he's trying to gather enough strength to get up. Instead of standing, he looks at me.

"They aren't telling us everything. And I'm too damned afraid to ask any questions."

"I'd be afraid, too. But maybe there's nothing to tell. Lots of people have cancer, get better, return to their normal lives."

"Right."

Always so healthy.

My worry bubbles to the surface and suddenly tears are filling my throat, my nose. I sniff them back. I certainly don't want to upset my father any more than he is.

"Are you okay?" he asks.

I rub my eyes with my fingers. "Yeah, I'm fine."

"You should go home, honey. Jan's here. I'll eat more, I promise. You need to be home."

I stare at the carpet, feel light-headed, numb. "I'm fine. Really. I want to stay and help you get better." When I look up, he shakes his head.

"I'd feel better if you went home. There's no need for both you and Jan to be here."

"No, I'll stay, help Jan."

He stares at me for a moment, worry filling his

gaze. "I'm going to try to do better, you'll see. You gave Jan a break. That's all she needed. You can always come back in a few weeks."

I do want to go home, yet I feel like shit for wanting to. "No, I'll stay."

"I think I'd do better if I knew you were home."

What can I say to that? My father asking me to leave. Maybe he just doesn't want me here.

"I'd feel better if I knew you were with Dave. He must miss you. The diagnosis shocked me. I'll try to eat more. And I'd feel more relaxed if you were home."

He forks mashed potatoes into his mouth, swallows. "See. We'll be fine."

I nod.

"You go home, honey. David must miss you."

Jan has just come home from the Skillys', and she and I are standing in the living room. Dad's in bed. I think she's had too much to drink, but it's difficult to tell with her.

"I'm going home in the morning," I say. I feel tense because deep down I know she's not going to like this news.

She looks at me as if I've told her hell froze over while she was at the Skillys'.

"You're what?"

"Dad ate dinner and we talked. He said he'd feel better if I went home. In fact, he said he wants me to go home. I'll come back in a few weeks."

"He ate?" Her eyes narrow and her lips flatten against each other. "He won't eat for me."

"He didn't eat a lot." I go back into the kitchen, stand at the stove, stir the spaghetti sauce that's been simmering an hour. After I called the airline, I made the sauce so I could leave an extra meal in the refrigerator.

I place the stained wooden spoon on the folded paper towel next to the stove. I hear Jan walk in and I turn around. She sits at the oak table.

"What's that smell?" She lifts her chin, sniffs the air, makes a face.

"I'm making spaghetti sauce for you." Why do I always lie to make people happy? I've never liked this about myself but can't seem to stop. The sauce isn't for her. It's for Dad because I want him to eat, get better, be healthy.

"This way you'll have meals for a few days."

"That's nice, but what about the other days? With all the work around here, I don't have time to cook."

"You can pick up Luby's takeout."

"It's hard for me to drive at night. And I don't like Luby's."

"You drove tonight and did okay." I turn back, pick up the spoon and stir the sauce. She clucks her tongue.

"That's different. Why are you going home?"

I want to say, *Because you are driving me crazy*, but I swallow back the words, take a deep breath and turn to her.

"Dad wants me to go home. He said so while we were having dinner. I can come back in a few weeks."

"I can't do this alone." She gestures toward the sink, the stove. "I need help."

Confusion wells in my chest. Now that the door is open, I don't think I can close it—stay here another day. If I can just get home for a few days, center myself then I'll come back, help her all I can.

"I'll come back in a week, really. I'll call the cleaning lady to come in more often. What would work for you? Twice or three times a week?"

"That's not the point!"

"I've run all the errands and the refrigerator is full. And the Skillys could help you."

She shakes her head, laughs cynically. "It's more

than that. I'm tired of the responsibility. And it's hard for me to drive him to radiation."

"It's only four miles. You don't even have to drive on a major street. Just do it for a week, then I'll be back."

"I get nervous with Stanley in the car. What would I do if something happens? Plus I have no rights when it comes to his health. No one wants to talk to an ex-wife. What if something really bad happens? I can't sign checks, do anything important."

I know it's difficult for her, but my father has asked me to go home, and I'm hoping this will make him feel better. I smile at Jan. "I'll come back in five days, I promise. You and Dad can have some time together."

"What if I need money?"

"Dad can sign checks. He paid a couple of bills today."

She shakes her head and I turn back to the sauce, stir it slowly. Two years ago my father sent Jennifer and me airline tickets to come to Las Cruces. I was surprised when he did this, yet flattered he wanted to spend time with us. Through the years we've seen each other sporadically, and he doesn't know my daughter very well.

For those three days we hiked in the desert, ate Mexican food at the Skillys' and talked. He kidded Jennifer about college, about boys, and I watched them laugh, have a good time. I was so happy we could be together.

The last day, while Jenny was watching a movie, Dad brought me to his desk, showed me where he kept all his important papers. Then he explained he'd made me executor of his will.

"But, Dad, you're healthier than I am," I said easily, and laughed.

"If I get really sick, just shoot me."

That afternoon we drove to the bank and I signed cards to be on his checking account.

"It's hard for me to drive him every day to radiation," Jan breaks in, brings me back to the kitchen.

"There's a program the nurse told me about. It helps people get to doctor's appointments. And really, Dad could probably drive himself to radiation."

"You know Stanley wouldn't like strangers driving him. And I don't want him to drive alone. I'd be too worried. *You* should stay."

She places her hands on the table, looks hard at me.

"Jan, he asked me to go home. I'll come back in a few days, I promise."

Her right hand comes up, cuts the air in front of her.

"You need to help your father. He's been a wonderful parent to you."

I think about the times—the holidays—when I didn't see him, when he was with Jan.

She never wanted me to have much to do with you kids.

I try to shake this thought away, but I can't. The first year David and I were married, after Dad divorced Jan, I called, asked him to come for Christmas, wanted us to be a family. Dad refused, said he'd already made plans. That February, I found out he and Jan had gone on a cruise.

Hurt swirls in my chest, gathers all my pushed-back emotions and makes a huge storm.

"Dad asked me to go. I've already told David." I picture myself in my kitchen, looking out the window at the sunrise.

"Husbands come and go. Your father is here."

I close my eyes and want to say that she, above all people, should know about husbands *coming and going*. But I swallow the words like flat, round communion wafers I saw one time when I went to church with a friend. I turn back to the spaghetti sauce, stir it once, watch it boil.

"I'm leaving early in the morning," I say finally. "I'll

come back in a few days. You'll be fine. There are left-overs from tonight." I gesture toward the refrigerator.

"Well, if something happens to Stanley."

I turn, look at her. "Why do you insist on saying that? My father has always been healthy, and I know he's going to get better! It's just going to take some time."

"If something happens to Stanley, I might take his car and drive back to Seattle. You know, take my time, stop at different places on the way. It would be good for me."

Her voice is so breathy I think about slapping her. Instantly I'm appalled at my anger.

"You *can't* drive him to radiation treatment, but you can drive to Seattle?" Confusion and anger melt together, wells in my throat, chest.

She leans back, her eyes wide. I've caught her and I'm ashamed of how good this makes me feel. My father is lying in bed, fighting cancer, and I'm trying to hurt the person who is going to take care of him for the next week.

"Well…that's a different kind of driving," she says, then gets up, pulls at the edge of her sweater and walks out of the room.

CHAPTER FIVE

Last night, after I did the dishes and packed, I made a reservation with Super Shuttle to pick me up and take me to the airport this morning because I knew Jan wouldn't drive me. She's barely speaking to me.

Now I'm waiting in the kitchen and my suitcase is by the front door. Earlier, I went into Dad's bedroom, told him goodbye and I'd be back in a week to help out. Then I folded my blankets and sheets, put them in the hall closet.

My father and Jan are sitting on the couch. Jan is resting her head on Dad's shoulder, and she just said something to him, but I couldn't make it out. He shifts and she's forced to sit up, turn to face him.

"Stanley, why can't we get married again?" Her voice is loud, not her Marilyn Monroe whisper.

My breath catches. What's she thinking? This isn't the time to get married, and they never got along anyway.

"We could have the ceremony here at the house. Then I could really take care of you."

Dad moves his head back and forth. Jan stands, looks at me, then goes to her bedroom.

"Dad went to a psychiatrist yesterday," I tell David. We are sitting in the family room and David is reading the newspaper. I've been home three days.

I was so surprised when Jan told me this afternoon about his trip to the psychiatrist yesterday. His regular doctor recommended the visit because he believes Dad is depressed.

"Right," David says, but doesn't look up.

I call Jan every day, and she tells me about her disasters: She got stuck in traffic; my father's radiation treatment took forever; it's difficult for her to sleep. She rarely tells me anything about how my father is coping, except today, when she described how my father sat in front of the psychiatrist and wouldn't say anything.

This morning I reassured her I'd be back in three days, that she can go home to Seattle if she wants when I get there. She gasped, said she couldn't possibly leave Stanley.

David told me yesterday I shouldn't call every day, but I feel guilty if I don't.

"David."

He lowers the newspaper, looks at me, smiles. "Yeah?"

"The doctor made arrangements for my father to see a psychiatrist because he thinks he's depressed. And now the psychiatrist wants him to go on Prozac."

David shakes his head. "I wouldn't take that stuff. I'm sure your father doesn't want to, either."

"But maybe it'll help him feel better."

"People should leave the guy alone." By *people* I know he means Jan and me.

"Maybe you're right. Dad did tell Jan that he wouldn't go back to the psychiatrist."

"See."

I close my eyes for a moment. "Honey?"

He looks up again. "Melinda, doesn't Jan exaggerate?"

"Yeah, but when I was there, he was pretty down."

"He's got a lot to think about, and I'd be down, too, if I had cancer and an uncertain future."

David is right. I think about Dad's health all the

time so I can imagine what he must be going through. More worry climbs over my shoulders, digs into my spine.

"Worrying's not going to help," David says.

I smile, realize my husband knows me pretty well. "It's not that easy. Plus, now I'm dealing with Jan."

The first time I met Jan, my father had just started dating her. It was around Christmas. I was still in junior high school, and Lena and I were supposed to spend holidays with him.

My mother was so angry that I was going to see my father, she would barely speak to me. The day before I left, she released her thunder, yelled she wanted me to stay home, that I was her daughter, and I should be with my mother for Christmas. Then she started ranting that I was a *traitor*, an ungrateful daughter. I felt ashamed and sad, torn between my parents, like a paper doll being ripped right down the middle.

Lena, seventeen, sided with my mother, told my father she didn't want to visit. She stood beside Mom at the airport, gloating, holding my mother's hand.

After I got to my father's small apartment, Dad and I drove over to Jan's house for dinner. When we walked in her living room, Donnie, then six, was sitting by the tree, begging to open another package. He saw us, stood and ran through the house, screaming he wanted to see Santa. Jan said nothing to her son, just smiled like everything was fine.

I couldn't get over how beautiful she was with her red lips and hair, her pretty eyes, long legs. After dinner we gathered in the living room and she handed me a small Christmas package. I peeled back the paper, found a robin's-egg-blue Revlon makeup kit with three little circles of lipstick, two eye shadows and a tiny brush. I'd been looking at the same one at the Rexall drugstore down the street from my mother's house, but it was too expensive for my thirteen-year-old babysitting budget.

I picked up the brush, then touched the Pink Passion circle of lipstick and dabbed it on my bottom lip. Suddenly emotion flooded my chest, my throat, and I burst into tears. The hurt over the way my mother had treated me pouring out.

Jan touched my shoulder. "This should be a happy day, Melinda," she whispered in her little-girl voice. "It's Christmastime."

I tried to smile but couldn't stop my tears.

"Melinda, stop crying." Dad sounded embarrassed at my display of emotion, my imperfect behavior.

Finally, I sniffed back my tears, felt as weak as a rag doll. And for the rest of the evening, I tried to act happy.

David clears his throat, shifts a little in his chair and looks at me.

"You look pretty tonight," he says.

I laugh, pull my hair behind my ear. "Oh, I'm a mess. But thanks."

"You know, we should take a trip. Today at lunch the guys were talking about the wine country in California. Would you like to go there?"

"Well, you know I like my wine." I laugh and so does he.

"Plan something. I'll call you from the office tomorrow and give you some dates that I can get away."

I nod, don't tell him that I feel I shouldn't even be thinking of going anywhere because of my father's condition. But I shake this negative thought away. My father is going to be fine, and David seems so happy right now, I don't want to ruin the mood. Dad will be better in a few months and David and I can take the trip, remind ourselves how worried we were a few months before.

"I'd like to go in late spring, when it's warm," I

say. "That would be fun. There'd be lots of wine, so there'd be lots of laughs."

He winks at me.

The phone rings and I startle. David looks up. "Are you going to get that?"

I nod.

Dad is in the Las Cruces hospital. He was taken there in an ambulance two days ago. When the phone rang the other night, it was Jan calling to tell me that he'd been admitted to the hospital because his bladder had suddenly shut down and the doctor had to insert a catheter. They were keeping him under observation because he'd complained of pain in his stomach.

That evening I hung up the phone and walked into the family room, told David the situation. Then I went back to the bedroom, stood in the middle of the room, didn't know what to do.

David followed me and suggested I go to Las Cruces the next day. I agreed, and he got my suitcase out, went on-line and bought another expensive airline ticket.

Since I've been here I've gone to the hospital twice a day. Yesterday, in a fit of anguish, I called David and gently asked him to come here, but he said he couldn't take the time off work. He's a partner in the firm, and they do have a lot of projects going on. I didn't say anything and he asked if I was angry. Before I could tell him I was okay, only disappointed that he always puts his job first, he explained he felt like he'd only be in the way with Jan here.

David's right. There's not even enough room for me.

"What am I going to do?" Jan whispers as she walks into Dad's kitchen, her arms crossed tightly.

The room is a disaster—dirty dishes, tea mugs, forks and spoons on the counters, in the sink. I have been at the hospital for hours, sitting with Dad, hoping Dr. Martinez will come in so I can talk to him. I've called his office, but he hasn't returned any of my calls.

"Dad's going to be okay," I say.

"But what am I going to do?" She stares at me. Her hair is sticking out in funny places—as if she combed it with an eggbeater, as my mother used to say. She's wearing the same outfit she's had on for two days—the lavender sweater, black pants and scarf, the one she was wearing when I picked her up from the airport.

"You could go home." I hold my breath, wait for her answer. For the past few days I've thought about Jan leaving, going back to Seattle.

"Home? Why would I go home?" She uncrosses her arms and then crosses them again, looks at me like I'm crazy.

"Maybe you'd be happier there. I know it's hard for you here."

She opens her mouth as if she's going to say something then closes it, and for some odd reason she reminds me of a fish.

"You could go home for a little while and then come back. You know, just take a break from all this."

"What would I do at home?"

"Relax. I'd call you every day." I think about bringing my father home from the hospital without Jan here. It would be so quiet, doable.

"If something happens to Stanley I don't know what I'll do."

I close my eyes, take a deep breath. "Nothing is going to happen to my father." I stand. "He's healthy. There's no reason why he won't come home and get better. I know he's going to beat this."

"I guess I could take Stanley's car and drive home, stay in motels on the way, try to relax."

"Yes. You could. I'll rent a car. That's not a bad idea. Then, when he's better you could drive back."

She uncrosses her arms, stares at her hands. "I can't go. How could I leave him?"

"We all can't live here forever." I point toward my bed on the floor in the corner of the dining room. Jan did suggest I sleep in my father's' bed, but for some reason I just can't do that.

"The condo's too crowded. If you go home for a little while David might come and help me."

"I could never desert Stanley." Jan's voice is hard, regular, the whisper gone.

I swallow back the steely taste that's seeping into my mouth. It's obvious she's not going to leave.

"I just think it would be better if you go home. You're miserable here."

"Are you trying to get rid of me?" She stares at me.

"No, it would just be easier for me," I say, and immediately regret it.

Her expression turns hard. "Yes, you are. And the way I've worked my guts out." She gets up, walks out of the kitchen.

Why couldn't I just keep my big mouth shut? I look around and hate the shape the kitchen is. I walk to the sink, begin throwing tea bags in the trash.

Five minutes later Jan pulls her large squeaky suitcase into the kitchen, her purse over her arm.

"What are you doing?"

She walks briskly through the kitchen, bumps into a chair, stops and resituates herself then heads for the garage. I follow her. I don't want her to be angry, tell my father that she's unhappy, that I tried to convince her to go home. He has enough to worry about.

She struggles to load her suitcase in the trunk, slams the lid then climbs in behind the wheel.

"Jan," I yell.

"You want me to leave, I'll leave," she yells out the window then starts my father's BMW, hits the garage door opener that's clipped to the visor and backs out. She drives down the street, and shock fills my entire body. While she doesn't do much around here except drink tea and make messes, I still don't want her to go this way. But I do get tired of taking care of two people, only one of which is ill.

I go back inside, stand at the sink and wonder if she'll come back. I look at the empty living room. For one short, hopeful moment, I think about being in my breakfast nook watching the beautiful sunrise.

CHAPTER SIX

Dad's hospital room is filled with warm winter sunlight. I'm standing by the window looking out at the parking lot where I parked the blue Saturn I rented two days ago after Jan left. I've called the Skillys three times to speak with Jan, but she won't talk to me. What I didn't realize when she marched through the kitchen, was that she'd also taken my father's wallet and Tag watch.

I press my hands against the windowsill, feel the cold from the outside and sigh. Exhaustion has settled in my legs, under my eyelids. I turn back to the hospital bed. Dad's asleep and he looks small, fragile.

When I was a kid, my father walked into our living room at night looking ten feet tall. Lena and I were usually sitting on the living room floor reading. He'd pat our heads and immediately ask where our mother was. Most times she was in the kitchen fixing dinner. Before Dad made his nightly entrance, my mother would wet a washcloth, wipe the streaks of dirt from our faces and tell us not to bother him when he got home.

"Your father has worked hard all day so we can have this nice life. I want the house and both of you perfect for him," she'd say. She did this until she decided she didn't want it so perfect and divorced him. That was after he found out about the bartender she'd met at a catered bridge party.

I walk to the edge of the hospital bed.

Dad opens his eyes.

"How are you?" I ask. According to one of the nurses, the doctor wants to keep him under observation for his stomach pain because they haven't been able to determine what's causing it.

"I'm okay." But he squeezes his eyes shut and moans.

"Dad, what's wrong?" I don't know why I ask this. He says the same thing every time.

"I need a pain pill."

"Are you sure?"

My father moans his answer.

I walk out to the nurses' station, stand by the counter and wait for the nurse who is always on duty at this time. She looks up, but doesn't smile, doesn't say anything.

"My father is asking for a pain pill." I feel a little like I'm in that movie with Shirley MacLaine and Debra Winger.

Sharon puts down her blue pen, lifts a paper in front of her face. I hear her tell the nurse behind her my father only wants a pain pill when I'm in his room. I have an urge to reach over the counter, grab her collar, pull her face close to mine and explain I'm only trying to help him, something she would probably do with her own father. But instead, I close my eyes, take a deep breath and remind myself I'm not a violent person, have never been and certainly don't want to be now.

My anger subsides a little, thank God, because if I did what I was thinking, I'm sure Sharon would call security. Then Jan would have proof that I'm the mean person she's telling the Skillys I am.

Mr. Skilly explained on the phone last night that Jan told them I insulted her, and she will not come back to the condo until I leave. I recounted our little scene in the kitchen, but when I was finished, he said he didn't want to get involved.

"Can my father have the pain pill, please?" I ask again, take another deep breath.

"I'll get it in a minute." She smiles a little.

"Thank you."

I turn away from the counter, walk back down the hall. The elevator opens and my father's doctor steps out.

"Dr. Martinez." I plunge toward him. He's walking in the opposite direction of Dad's room.

He stops, faces me. "Yes?"

"May I speak with you? I'm Stanley Howard's daughter."

"Oh, yes." He extends his hand and I take it.

"I've called you at your office."

"I have quite a few emergencies." He gestures down the hall then smiles.

"I can wait for you." I point to the bench by the elevator. "I just want to discuss when my father will be well enough to leave the hospital."

"Give me a few minutes."

I sit on the hard bench next to the elevator, lean against the shiny white wall. I'm so happy we're going to talk. I want to find out when my father can come home. I open my purse and check my phone. David has called me twice this morning. The day Jan left, I explained to him what happened. And even though he didn't say much, I could tell he was disgusted.

Twenty minutes later, I look at my watch. I'm still waiting for Dr. Martinez. I stand, pick up my purse, walk around the corner. Maybe he forgot I'm here. Across from another nurses' station, I see him. He and a young, dark-haired nurse are in a corner, talking. She smiles and he laughs, leans closer to her.

Anger builds in my chest.

"Dr. Martinez."

He glances at me, surprise in his expression. Then he steps forward, and I close the space between us.

"Dr. Martinez, I've been waiting to talk to you. Did you forget?" My gaze drifts to his gold wedding band.

"I'm sorry," he says to the nurse. "I'll be just a minute."

She smiles sympathetically, turns and walks down the hall, goes into the first room on her left. For a quick moment, I want to follow her, touch her shoulder. When she turns around, I want to tell her that this doctor forgot about me. But what good would that do?

I look at him. "I want to know when my father will be able to come home."

He rubs his face, looks exhausted. "Your father needs to go into a nursing home. His health is getting worse."

This suggestion stuns me—my father, tall, always healthy, so independent, in a nursing home? I shake my head.

"My father won't go into a nursing home."

"I don't think it's a good idea for him to go home. Your mother said he wouldn't eat or drink when she was there. When he came to the hospital, he was dehydrated. And he has scar tissue in his urethra. So he needs the catheter."

"She's not my mother, she's his ex-wife."

He looks at me oddly.

"My mother and father are divorced, Dad married Jan and then divorced her."

"He either needs to go in a nursing home, or have someone help him with hospice care because of the cancer, the depression."

"I tried to get him to drink water, really, I even bought straws and I cooked. I don't want him to stay alone, either, but I don't live here." I hug myself, feel numb, desperate.

"He can't stay in the hospital much longer. This isn't a long-term facility."

"He was so healthy before all this."

"He's a very sick man," the doctor says.

"Is he going to get better?" I ask, hold my breath, and right away I wish I hadn't asked this question. I want to believe that once he gets out of here, he'll be all right.

He shakes his head. "I think your father is dying."

Dying?

I close my eyes and my chest begins to ache. I take a deep breath, push my feelings back.

"I'm sorry," Dr. Martinez says.

I look at him. His gaze is filled with sympathy.

"You said *think*. I mean, there might be a chance he'll get better?"

"There's always a chance."

"Can he stay here for a day or two? I need to talk to my husband about all this."

The doctor puts his hand on my shoulder and I feel his warmth.

"You might think about taking him home with you. You could get hospice care. That's what some of my patients have done."

"Home with me?"

"Yes, then you could take care of him, be in your own environment."

"I need to talk to my husband. Thank you." I turn, walk down the hall.

I think your father is dying.

I go into Dad's room. He's lying on his side, facing the wall.

I sit in the chair by the door, stare at the wall. A nursing home! A memory floats in—afternoon, my parents driving back from visiting my mother's father in a sad, smelly nursing home right outside of Austin. Lena and I were in the back seat, quiet, sleepy from the warmth filling the car.

"I'd rather die than go into something like that," Dad said to my mother. She nodded, her expression grim.

Later that afternoon, he came into the backyard carrying a yellow rosebush. I was lying on the grass, warm spring sunlight drizzling over me. His white T-shirt was stretched hard against his chest and his tanned biceps. He began digging a small circle that turned into a deep hole.

"Melinda, you look just like your mother sitting there," he said, didn't smile. "Don't ever get old, honey, because it's no fun."

I cover my face with my hands and cry.

Dying.

The feeling I should pray comes over me, but I can't. I haven't done that since my friend Vanessa was killed in the car wreck, and I prayed it wasn't true. Three days later her mother asked me to pack Vanessa's things. After I finished, I studied the boxes and cried hard, amazed she could be here one minute, lying on her twin bed laughing, and then just disappear. Alone with shadows and memories of a good friend, I quit believing because nothing made sense to me.

"Melinda, why are you crying?"

Dad has turned over and his face is filled with concern. I get up, walk to the bed and sit on the edge. He places his hand on mine and I'm surprised at how warm his skin is.

"Don't cry, honey."

I try to stop, but can't. Ragged sobs race out of my body.

"Honey, why are you crying?"

"Dr. Martinez says you have to leave the hospital in two days."

Dad nods. "That's good. I want to get out of here."

"He told me it would be better for you to go into a nursing home."

Dad's expression grows masklike. "I don't have a choice?"

"He said you could come to Texas and stay with us."

"How would I get there?"

I shake my head. "I don't know."

Dad closes his eyes and so do I.

CHAPTER SEVEN

Dad's answering machine is blinking. I put my
purse on the counter, push the button.

"Hi, it's Elizabeth. Just checking on you. David
gave me your father's number. Hope everything is
okay. Call me if you have time."

I lean against the counter, start to dial her
number but the doorbell rings. At the door I look
through the peephole. Mr. Skilly is standing on the
porch.

Winter sunshine tumbles in through the open
door. I realize my eyes must be swollen and puffy
from crying so hard. "Hi. Come in," I say, try to sound
upbeat.

Mr. Skilly shakes his head, crosses his arms. "I
better not. I've got some errands."

We stand for a moment in sunshine and silence.

"How's your father?"

"The doctor said Dad can't stay in the hospital

anymore." The words slip out, wind around us. "I don't know what I'm going to do."

"He's coming home?" Mr. Skilly's expression softens a little and he uncrosses his arms.

"No, the doctor said he has to go to a nursing home or come home with me if we get hospice. I certainly don't want to put him in a nursing home, but I don't know how to get him to my house."

Tears begin to build in my throat and I swallow them back. I want to tell Mr. Skilly what else the doctor said, that he thinks Dad is dying, but I don't know how to say this to his best friend. Plus, if I say the words, it will make what the doctor told me more real.

"That's awful. Poor Stan." His expression grows tighter as he continues to stare at me.

"I'm worried, Mr. Skilly."

"I know you must be." He reaches out to touch my shoulder, but pulls back, pats his jacket pocket, brings out a wallet.

"Jan asked me to give you this. She packed it by mistake."

"Thanks." I turn the brown wallet over in my hand, then look at him. Does he really believe my father's wallet got into her suitcase by mistake?

"I want to take my father back to Texas, but I'm not sure he's strong enough to fly on a commercial airplane. And he certainly can't make a long car trip."

"This is tough." He rubs his face. "I just don't know anymore. Your dad was so strong a few weeks ago. He was always so..." His voice catches and before I can reach out and pat his arm, say thank-you for caring about him, he turns and heads down the sidewalk.

For a moment I think about running after him, but I know he's probably embarrassed that he was about to cry in front of me. When he disappears around the corner, I go inside. At first, Mr. Skilly seemed angry, and I wonder if Jan told him I stole the handicapped placket out of Dad's car. Yesterday afternoon I saw Dad's car parked in one of the hospital handicapped parking spaces with the placket hanging on the mirror. Weeks ago, I went to the motor vehicle department and got the permit for my father after his doctor recommended it.

The combination of Jan parking where she shouldn't, keeping my father's car and not speaking to me made me mad, so I reached in, grabbed the placket and shoved it in my purse.

Now, I feel like an idiot for doing that. I find my purse, pull out the blue sign. If I see my father's car I'll hang it back on the mirror, and let it be on Jan's conscience if she takes a handicapped person's parking space.

In the corner of the dining room, where my blankets are, I kick off my shoes and lie down. I'm still dressed in a black turtleneck and jeans, but I'm too tired to care. It's only two-thirty, but the drapes are still closed so the room is dark.

I rub my forehead. Would Dad be happy at our house? It would be easier to stay here, but if I do that, I know Jan will want to come back. I need to call David, talk to him about all this. Yet, right now, I'm so exhausted I can't even think about talking to anyone.

I think your father is dying.

The words pulse through my thoughts, and I tell myself this is not going to happen. My father is going to pull through this, and a few months down the road, he'll be fine.

"I had a dream," I say to David.

"Who are you, Martin Luther King?" he asks, then laughs.

Despite the way I feel, I laugh at his silly joke. I dialed David's office number a moment ago.

"No, listen. I fell asleep and I had a dream about a small airplane flying across the sky. My father and I were inside, happy, coming to Texas. The dream felt so real it woke me up. That's when I knew I should rent a plane and bring my father home."

"Rent a plane?"

"I have a feeling I need to do this. David, the doctor said he thinks Dad is dying. Being at our house might help him."

There is this deep silence between us that is thick, almost touchable, and I imagine David sitting at his desk, his expression serious.

"Melinda, have you asked your father if he wants to come here?"

"The doctor said he can't stay in the hospital, and I don't want him to go to a nursing home. A long time ago, he said he never wanted to go in a nursing home. I can't stay here, David. What if Jan wants to come back? If I bring him home, I think he'll get better."

"Then you should bring him here."

"Thank you. I knew you'd be okay with it."

"The plane, how much would it cost?"

"I don't know." I walk over to the desk, open

Dad's checkbook and look at the balance—seven thousand dollars.

I guess for months he hasn't done anything with his retirement checks.

"He's got the money, David. Elizabeth is there, and a while back she said she'd help me. The doctor recommended hospice, but maybe we won't need it. I mean, the doctor did say *thinks*. I remember that. Doctors don't always know everything."

I am sitting across from a Las Cruces hospital social worker. A moment ago she came into the hallway, introduced herself as Anna and guided me into her small, windowless office. She is tiny, about twenty-six, with a Crest-white smile, and for the last few minutes I have relaxed in her kindness.

After I hung up with David, I called Elizabeth, asked her what I should do. She suggested I contact the hospital social worker and he or she would help me.

"I understand," Anna says again. "Many of our patients' families want to be home. And there's always a way to get patients to where they need to be."

"I'm not working right now, so I can take care of my father. My friend, who lives close by, is a nurse."

Anna nods. "It sounds like you have a support system at home."

"I do." I imagine my father in the back bedroom of our home and wonder again if taking him to Texas is for the best.

"It's not a good idea to stop your entire life for your father. Try to keep the same routine, that sort of thing." She smiles, reminds me a little of my Jenny. I miss my daughter. I tried to call her yesterday, but she didn't answer her cell, and I didn't want to leave a message about how sick her grandfather is, so I just said hi, that I'd call her back soon.

"You said you taught. My mother's a teacher," Anna says.

I smile. "I'm not sure I'll continue teaching."

"Does your father want to go to Texas with you?"

"Yes." I think about his expression when I told him I thought it was the best thing to do. His eyes went blank for a moment, then he nodded, said he'd come home with me. I squeezed his hand, said I thought everything would be okay.

"Were you taking care of your father before he was admitted to the hospital?"

"Sometimes. His ex-wife did, too."

"That would be depressing to have to depend on

your ex-wife when you're sick. If he's agreeable to going to your home, I can make arrangements to get him there. We have patients who travel on medical jets all the time. It's expensive, though."

I think about my dream, how happy we were flying, going home. "How much will it cost?"

"Let's see." Anna clicks the computer mouse. "Yes, we usually use United Medical Air Service. You want to take him to Dallas?"

"The Dallas Fort Worth Airport." I feel a little dazed that I'm actually doing this.

She picks up the phone, punches in numbers, explains the situation to the person on the other end. A few moments later she hangs up, looks at me.

"It's six thousand dollars to fly your father to Fort Worth."

"One way?" I say stupidly.

"Yes." Anna hands me the notepaper she's been writing on. It has the name and number of the person she just talked to, and in big print, $6,000.

"Is there another way?"

"Only a commercial airline and your father isn't strong enough for that."

It's so much money. Will Dad be upset when he finds out how much I spent?

"So," Anna says. "Mr. Galante said he can make arrangements to fly your father day after tomorrow."

"Okay." I stand, put the note in my purse. "I'll call him as soon as I get home. I just want a little time to think about this."

CHAPTER EIGHT

"I made the arrangements for Dad."

I called David as soon as I finished talking with Mr. Galante from the medical flight service. That was after I came back to the condo, sat on the couch and thought about what it would be like to have my father living at our house.

"You did?" My husband's voice sounds thin, high, not like him at all. I guess now the idea of my father living at our house till he gets better is sinking in.

"You sound surprised."

"No, I'm fine."

"Is it okay?"

"Sure."

"We're flying in on Wednesday. Can you come and help me? You could fly home with us."

I hear him shuffling papers. I want David to say he'll come here, for moral support, and to tell me everything is going to be okay.

"Melinda, I have two deadlines right now. I have to close them, but I'll get things ready for you and Stan."

His answer is what I expected, yet I was hoping he'd switch his priorities to my father, me.

"Mr. Galante said that it's the same price no matter who flies to Texas."

"I have three projects going. I'm sorry, you'll be okay and then you'll be home."

"Right." I can barely say the word, but I know he has to work. I just wish sometimes he would not put so much importance on it. I look around the kitchen, try to fight the feelings that are blistering under my skin. Work comes before anything else for David.

"How are you getting to the airport?"

"I'll take a taxi to the hospital, then an ambulance will take us there."

"Should I pick you up at the airport?"

"No, Mr. Galante arranged for an ambulance to be there."

"Melinda."

"Yes." I try to hide my anger.

"I'm sorry I have so many projects."

I hear the guilt in his voice, want to say, *Well,*

then come. Think of us instead, but I don't. David's job has provided us a nice life, and I'd feel guilty for complaining.

"It's okay. We'll be home day after tomorrow. And then everything will be fine. I have a feeling Dad's going to get better."

Yet the feeling of dread that I haven't let myself think about, surfaces, coils in my chest. I push it away. My father is going to be one of those people who beats cancer.

"It'll be nice to have you home," David says.

"It will be nice to be home."

"Make sure you turn his hot water heater down, lock all the doors and get his car back."

I laugh. Some things never change. "I thought of all those. I want to leave the condo just the way Dad would want it so it'll be okay until he comes home. I'll call the Skillys, ask them to tell Jan I want his car back. She can rent a car."

"You haven't heard from her?"

"No, she still won't talk to me."

"Jesus, that woman."

"It'll be okay. I'll get everything done and then we'll be home."

We say goodbye. I walk into my father's bedroom.

A water glass still sits on his nightstand, red straw standing at attention. I rub my forehead, wish my husband were here, feel a bit bruised.

Even though David and I are alike in many ways, we don't always agree. I've never understood how he can put work before everything else. At times, he reminds me so much of my father, wanting everything perfect, working so hard to get it that way. One day, after we had a terrible fight, his sister told me that when he was young he would sit at the kitchen table and work on model cars for hours at a time until they were just right. Even in college, he worked harder than anyone I knew. And now—he's so focused on his job that nothing turns his head, not even my father's illness or my needs.

I'm sitting in the kitchen waiting for Mr. Skilly to bring back Dad's car. I called last night, and he answered the phone, so I asked him to tell Jan we're leaving tomorrow. He called twenty minutes ago, said he was coming over with the car.

Yesterday, between trips to the hospital, I cleaned the condo, then went across the street to the neighbors and asked if they would keep an eye on the place. Ellen sat next to me on the couch and really listened as I told her about Dad. Just talking helped me feel a little better, but then I came home and couldn't sleep last night. I kept thinking about how, before Dad's illness someone would tell me a family member was ill, and I'd listen but I never connected.

Now I will.

This morning I called Elizabeth. She said she thought I was making the right decision and that made me feel better.

The doorbell rings. When I open the door I smile. Mr. Skilly is standing on the small porch. He's holding my father's car keys in his right hand.

"Come in," I say, happy to have someone to talk to.

"No, I can't."

He hands me the keys and the metal feels cold against my skin.

"Thank you for bringing back Dad's car. I want to leave everything the same so when he comes home…"

Mr. Skilly looks toward the street, as if he's not listening to me.

"I'm sorry. You're in a hurry. I'll drive you home." I walk onto the porch. He holds up his hand, shakes his head.

"No need for that, I'll walk home."

"Really?"

"Yeah." He crosses his arms in a way that makes my stomach sink. "You know, your father's like a brother to me."

"Dad says that same thing about you." My father actually has never said this to me. But he looks so sad right now. Many times Mr. Skilly and Dad hiked in the mountains and went on camping trips together. One time, they navigated a canoe down the Green River in Utah for a week. My father called me after, told me about the trip, how much fun they had.

"He really thinks a lot of you, Mr. Skilly. Maybe you could go to the hospital and see him before we leave tomorrow."

"I'm not one for hospitals."

His response startles me, and I want to say, *Well neither am I*, but I don't. I have known this man since I was a teenager and I don't want to hurt his feelings.

"When are you leaving?" he asks, seems so distracted.

"We're leaving early tomorrow morning."

"It's terrible, the way you've been treating Jan."

I blink, feel like I've been slapped in the face.

"Well…I really didn't treat her any *way*. She just…she walked out."

"She was crying last night. And now, taking your father away like this…it just isn't right."

"I called her, she won't talk to me. And I'm trying to help my father. I had this dream about taking him home," I say, and when his expression changes, I immediately wish I hadn't said anything.

"A dream. What are you talking about?"

"It's a long story."

"How could you tell Jan she can't go to the hospital?"

"What?" I look at him, feel like a bucket of cold water has been thrown on me. "That's a lie. I never told her she couldn't go to the hospital. Did she tell you she stole my father's watch along with his wallet? The woman is crazy! How could she take his watch and not give it back?"

His face flushes more. "How could you throw her out after all she's done for your father?" He takes a step back as if he's leaving.

"Wait a minute." I grab his sleeve. "I never threw her out! She left because she got mad, acted like a little kid."

He shakes his head, looks at my hand and I let go.

"I'm not getting into this with you."

"Then why the hell did you bring it up? I'm doing my best here. You haven't even gone to see Dad at the hospital and he's supposed to be your best friend." Right away I'm sorry for saying this. What would my father think? But I'm so tired of everyone telling me what I *should* be doing, yet not helping me.

Mr. Skilly shakes his head, turns and walks down the sidewalk to the street. At the street he stops, and I hope he'll turn around, tell me he knows Jan's a nutcase, impossible to deal with. But he rounds the corner and disappears.

My head pounds and I close my eyes against the thumping. I sit in the lawn chair by the window, feel numb. God only knows what other lies Jan told the Skillys about me.

Moments later, I stand, go to Dad's car and get in. The ashtray is full of cigarette butts smeared with red lipstick. I turn the key in the ignition, open all four windows. Stiff winter air fills the car as I put it in gear and drive down the street. When I reach the corner of Arroyo Grande and 17th, I pass Mr. Skilly, want to stop and try to explain to him again what really happened, but I keep my gaze straight ahead. I don't think he'd listen anyway.

For fifteen minutes I drive the streets, then I stop at Smith's Grocery Store because the smell of cigarettes is so strong it's making me nauseated. I empty the ashtray in the cement trashcan by the door. I had no idea Jan smoked. I go back to the condo, and lock the garage.

With Dad's suitcase open, I fold three shirts, his jeans, find tennis shoes, six pairs of underwear, socks and two pairs of blue pajamas. I place everything carefully—perfectly—in the suitcase, the way he would want it.

When I'm finished packing my things, I lie on the couch with a thin blanket over me. The "Dr. Phil Show" blares through the room, and I think about going home.

CHAPTER NINE

I slide the drape back and look out to the dark street. I didn't get much sleep last night. The taxi company promised to have someone here by four forty-five. A few minutes ago, I called them to make sure they wouldn't be late. In a few hours my father and I will be at my house.

I stare out the window. Headlights peek around the corner, illuminate the street, and my heart begins to race. I click on the porch light and a crayon-yellow taxi stops in front of the condo. The cab-driver gets out, walks up the sidewalk.

"I have these suitcases," I say as I pull the second one out onto the porch, feel the cold air on my face.

"No problem." The driver picks up both suitcases and heads toward the cab. I shut off the light, close and lock the door. In the back seat of the taxi, I see a blue-and-cream-colored Madonna glued to the lid of the ashtray.

The taxi driver climbs in, looks at me.

"I need to go to the Las Cruces Hospital," I say.

"Sure."

The man starts the taxi, glances in the rearview mirror at me. He looks like Al Pacino with his big dark eyes and thick hair.

"So early to the hospital?"

"My father's sick."

He nods, turns around in Dad's driveway and then we begin gliding down the street past dark, sleeping houses, the Smith's Grocery Store where I dumped Jan's cigarette butts. I imagine her sitting in the driver's seat of Dad's BMW lighting a Marlboro, smoke curling around her.

Soon we stop in the bright hospital parking lot and I get out before the driver does.

"Thank you." I dig in my wallet for the money I owe him.

He climbs out, goes to the trunk and places both suitcases beside me. I hand him a twenty.

"Keep the change." The fare is only ten-fifty, but I'm so relieved to be here on time, to be one step closer to home, I want to pay him more.

"Thank you." He studies the hospital tower. "I hope it goes well for you and your father."

"I hope so, too."

He folds the bill twice and it disappears into his breast pocket. "I'll help you with the suitcases."

I shake my head. "That's okay, I can get them."

"No." He grips the handles and walks with me across the parking lot.

It is so quiet the scuff of our shoes against the rough, dark asphalt fills the air. On the fourth floor, I lead the way down the quiet hall. At Dad's room, I face the taxi driver.

"Thank you for your help. This is my father's room."

Suddenly the man wraps his arms around me. My arms stay glued to my sides. Then just as quickly, he steps back, looks at me intently.

"God loves you and your father."

"Really?"

"Yes, he loves everyone, even the birds in the trees. You believe that, don't you?" He touches my arm, as if to prod me into saying I do.

"I don't know," I say, but inside I think he's wrong.

"You will, everybody finds out in due time that God loves them, even the little birdies in the trees. Tweet, tweet." Then he smiles.

I nod. The man seems a little insane.

He turns and walks down the hallway. Suddenly, I want to run after him, tap him on the shoulder and clarify that I don't believe in anything, that I haven't for a long time—that I've known there is no God or anything else since Vanessa died and I stood in our dorm room, looked around and wondered where she went. I have never figured out how any God could take her away from her mother, me, the world.

As if he can feel what I'm thinking, the driver stops, turns toward me and throws me a peace sign, smiles and then disappears around the corner.

Gripping the suitcases, I walk into Dad's room. The overhead lights are on and an older woman with short dark hair is wiping Dad's face with a white wash-cloth. His hair has been slicked down in an odd way, someone has shaved him, and his expression is waxy.

"Hi, Dad. Are you ready to go?" To my surprise, I feel a zing of excitement in the pit of my stomach about going home.

The nurse steps back and Dad looks at me.

"We're leaving in a little bit."

He nods and I can see he has a tiny shaving nick under his chin.

"We'll be home soon."

He presses his lips together, as if he's holding back something he really wants to say.

The nurse smiles at me. And I read her badge. Elizabeth. Nurse's Aide.

"You have the same name as my friend," I say, feel hurt in my chest because my father won't talk to me.

"Oh, that's nice." She straightens the items on her cart, then leans over and places her small brown hand on my father's shoulder.

"Mr. Howard, you are so lucky to have such a nice daughter to take you home with her. Have a good trip."

"Thank you," Dad says.

Elizabeth pushes her cart out to the hall, and I sit in the chair next to his bed.

"Ma'am?"

I look toward the door. Elizabeth stands by the doorjamb. She motions me to her. I get up, go over and we walk into the hall.

"Your father, he's mad at you?" she whispers the question.

"I'm not sure. Did he say something?"

The only time I remember my father being angry with me was when I was ten and I took his car keys off his dresser, went out to the garage and turned on the ignition and listened to the radio for an hour. I don't know why I did this. Maybe I saw something on TV, I'm not sure. But he found me, ordered me out of the car. He didn't yell, yet he looked at me with a cold anger. I said I was sorry, but he just turned away.

"Don't worry," Elizabeth says, "he'll be okay. My mama was mad at me, too, when she was sick. They take their illness out on the person who they love the most. You're doing the right thing, taking him home."

"I hope so." *The person they love the most.* I'm not sure this is true. I always thought the person my father loved the most was Jan or maybe Lena because she needed him so much.

"Don't worry, things will be better at home." She smiles, grips the metal handle of her cart and walks down the hall.

We are riding in one of those red square ambulances with white printing on the sides. Fifteen minutes ago the paramedics came into my father's room, put him on a gurney, then all of us walked downstairs.

Now, Dad is hooked to a blood pressure monitor and oxygen is nearby. Even though we are moving slowly, the ambulance sways a little as we go around a corner. The paramedic picks up Dad's medical chart, leafs through it.

"Says here your father's allergic to milk products."

"Really?" I look at Dad. His eyes are closed.

The paramedic nods, points to the chart resting on his knees. "Yeah, says it right here."

"Dad, are you allergic to milk?"

"No." He stays under the safety of his closed eyelids.

"Probably best to let him eat what he wants."

Dad winces and the paramedic continues to read the chart. Soon we stop and I look out the small window, see part of the airport.

"We're here, Mr. Howard." The paramedic unwraps the blood pressure cuff.

Dad looks at me, then quickly closes his eyes again.

The ambulance's back doors open like wings. The driver motions me forward, helps me out, then pulls our suitcases down.

I take a deep breath. The dry early morning air

is still. A bit of pink sunrise edges the gray clouds. When Jenny and I visited Dad, he and I took a walk one morning about this time. We got up early, drank a little coffee, then took off.

I face east. More sunrise ribbons—out in tiny strands—confetti-like, as if there's a celebration and no one has told me about it. I breathe in again, fill my lungs with the air of the peaceful morning, a new beginning. The last day of our trip, Dad took Jenny and me to Ruidoso early in the morning, and we wandered into a small chapel. The altar of the church was filled with streams of pink light from the stained-glass windows.

My father and I sat in the first pew as Jenny roamed around, touched the holy water, stared at the small statues.

"It's so beautiful," I said.

"It is."

"Dad, do you believe in all this?" I gestured toward the altar, wanted some sort of an answer. The last time I was in a church was for Vanessa's funeral.

"I do when it looks like this."

My heart softens a little with the memory. We were so happy that day, so full of hope. I look up at the sky decorated with fresh sunlight.

I'm going home.

I turn, watch them take Dad out of the ambulance. His eyes are still closed. I wish he would open them, look around and remember our morning in the church, how happy we were.

I walk toward the plane, stop, look at the sky one more time and drink in its beauty.

The pull of gravity pushes me down a little as the plane takes off. The male nurse has the oxygen mask over Dad's mouth and nose. He's lying on the airplane gurney, in the middle, where seats have been removed. A moment ago the nurse announced Dad's blood pressure is low.

I grip the armrest and look out the window, watch as the airport grows smaller, then disappears. We float toward the sun and the plane fills with pink light.

"Would you like a soft drink or juice?" the female nurse asks.

I turn around. "Any wine?"

She startles a little at my question, looks at the other nurse. "Do we have wine?"

He shakes his head.

"I was just kidding. I don't want anything, but

thank you." The plane climbs, bumps up and down with the turbulence. I keep holding on to the armrests, focus on the pewter sky, the beauty of the colors. Life, at times, is elegant, and other times it's so confusing.

"Are you okay?" the male nurse asks.

"Yes, I'm fine. Just a little nervous." I press my forehead on the cool double window, watch as we continue to climb, flying over snowy mountains far below.

We have landed at the Fort Worth airport. The male nurse opens the airplane door. I stare out the window. It is raining. I was hoping David would be waiting for us, too, but he isn't.

I scan the area again, wish David would drive up in his familiar Avalon. Yet I know this won't happen. If he were going to meet us, he would have told me.

The New Mexico nurses unload Dad from the airplane, rush him to the waiting ambulance. I go down the stairs and cold raindrops tap the top of my head. The paramedics position Dad in the ambulance. I climb in, make sure we have both suitcases.

"Dad, we're here."

"Yeah, we are." He looks at me. I smile and he nods.

The new paramedic is another good-looking young man with a serious expression and big shoulders. He wraps a blood pressure cuff around Dad's right arm and Dad opens his eyes.

"How are you, sir?"

"I'm doing okay."

"That's good." He takes Dad's blood pressure and notes it on the chart, then sits back. "That plane ride was probably real smooth compared to the roads in Texas. We've got the worst roads in the world," he says to me.

"I know."

"But we'll get you there in one piece. Safe and sound." He reads the first page of Dad's records and grimaces, and I'm happy my father can't see his expression.

Ten minutes later, we park in front of our house. Dad has not moved for the entire ride. The paramedics open the large back doors, pull out our suitcases, then take my father's gurney down from the ambulance. I climb out and, in the middle of the street, I rummage through my purse looking for my keys. I find them and they jingle in the light winter rain.

Before I can get my key in the lock, the door

opens. David, standing in the doorway, smiles at me. I'm so surprised that he stayed home from work, I pull back a little, then feel elated that he's here. He steps onto the porch, then sees my father on the gurney. For one quick moment his expression changes to one I've never seen before, but he recovers quickly and smiles again.

"Hey, Stan, you better come in out of the rain."

Dad opens his eyes, rises a little on his elbow. "Hey, Dave, how you doing?"

David goes into the house first, shows the attendants down the hall to the extra bedroom. I hear him and my father talking about the flight, the rain.

I walk into the kitchen, sigh, fill a glass with water and drink it slowly. Out the kitchen window, I watch as the paramedics collapse the gurney, put it back in the ambulance. Both men climb in the front and drive away.

The pansies and the ground are slick with rain. I imagine the daffodil bulbs underneath and wonder how many will come up this spring. A moment later David walks into the kitchen and smiles at me.

"Your father's settled in bed."

"Thanks for being here."

"I was sitting in my office this morning, thinking

about you and your dad coming home, so I rearranged some appointments. I'll have to go back this afternoon. You okay?"

"Yeah, I'm fine now that I'm home." I look around the kitchen, feel comfort and smile. "You know, I've got a feeling everything is going to be all right."

CHAPTER TEN

Elizabeth and I sit on the couch in the family room. My father is in bed in the back bedroom. David left an hour ago for the office. He explained again he has a lot to catch up on and he'll probably be home late. I'm so happy he was here when we arrived, grateful he thought about us.

"Did you talk to your dad about signing with hospice?" Elizabeth asks.

I shake my head. "Do you still think it's a good idea?" I sigh, rub my forehead.

"Yes, I do."

I want so much for my father to be healthy, to beat his illness. Deep down, I'm afraid if he decides to go with hospice, he'll give up.

"Dad's been so depressed. Did I tell you his doctor sent him to a shrink?"

"A lot of people who are diagnosed with cancer get depressed. Would you like me to talk to him?"

"I'm not sure." I hug myself, wonder what the right thing to do is.

"I'm sorry, Melinda."

"He just seems so shut down since he decided it was okay to come here. Maybe he's mad at me. I don't know."

Elizabeth gestures to Dad's medical file on the coffee table. "I've looked at his records. When prostate cancer metastasizes to the bone, usually the cancer is unstoppable. You and your father will need some help. One of us should talk to him."

Unstoppable.

My father was unstoppable before this. He was always determined, did things perfectly just a few months ago. And, for the first time, I realize life can turn on a dime. Instead of volunteering at the local library, a daughter has to talk to a nurse about hospice care for her father.

"If you think it's for the best." My voice is thin, scared.

Elizabeth's expression stays calm.

"Other people have been diagnosed with cancer and they seem to do just fine, live for a long time. Dad will do that."

"He might."

"What will you say when you talk to him?"

"I'll explain the program, then the patient decides if they want to go with hospice." Concern fills her gaze. "Melinda, hospice will help you with so many things, you can keep him at home the entire time. He won't ever have to go in the hospital again."

"Okay." Dad hates hospitals. Elizabeth and I stand, and I'm resolved that life is going to get better. Dad will eat, get stronger, beat this thing. "I'm sure he's awake."

Elizabeth goes into his room and I wait just inside the doorway. Dad is lying on the bed, in his pajamas with his hands folded on top of his chest. When David and I moved to this house, I decorated this room simply, leaving the walls white, putting a plain oak nightstand next to the bed. The last thing I did was hang a Georgia O'Keeffe print of a church, much like the one we visited in Ruidoso, on the wall across from the bed. I felt so connected to my father that day.

"Mr. Howard."

Dad looks at Elizabeth who is standing at the foot of his bed. She smiles.

"Mr. Howard, I'm a nurse with Fort Worth

Hospice and a friend of Melinda's. I came to talk to you about signing with our organization."

"I gave at the office."

Elizabeth laughs.

"Dad!"

"Would you like to talk about signing with hospice? We can offer you some helpful services, filing insurances and making sure you're never in pain. Do you know anything about hospice?"

He shifts his attention to me. His expression is a study in disappointment. I want to grab Elizabeth's hand, pull her out of the bedroom and tell her we need more time. But before I can do this Dad sits up a little.

"Will it help Melinda? Make things easier?"

"Don't worry about me, Dad. Think about yourself, do what you want." I take two steps into the room. I want him to say he won't sign with hospice, that there's no need to do this because he feels better today and tomorrow he's going to feel great.

"I don't want to be a problem for Melinda, so I guess if hospice will help, then I'll sign."

"We need to go over the paperwork—I'll explain what we can do for you and your family, then we'll complete the forms."

"Can he change his mind if he wants to?" I ask, feel panicky.

"Of course. Some people have done that." Elizabeth smiles at me. "Melinda, it'll be okay."

Dad sits up more and swings his legs over the edge of the bed. "Which papers do I have to sign?"

And my heart sinks a little more.

Dad signed the hospice papers a few minutes ago, then handed them back to Elizabeth.

"I'm tired," he says, lies back on the bed.

"I'll see you in a few days, Mr. Howard." Elizabeth takes his hand, shakes it, lets go. Dad's gaze drifts to the window.

I follow Elizabeth down the hall to the kitchen. I feel a little numb, weird. We stand at the counter. She puts copies of the signed papers into a blue pocket folder and hands it to me.

"When you get time, you should go through this folder. There's lots of information, telephone numbers, instructions about what you should do if there's an emergency."

I nod, feel more dazed, light-headed.

"Are you okay?"

"Yeah, fine. It's just…this is such a big step. I

thought about hospice in New Mexico, but now it's so real."

"We'll help you and your dad."

"He seems a little bit better since he got here."

"Patients have good days, bad days. Sometimes the caregivers are the ones who really get worn out. We can get you help. Also, there's a counselor and a minister who work with hospice. They'll come out—"

"No."

I think about Vanessa's funeral. How the minister said things happen for good reasons. That day, after his sermon, I went up to him, asked him what *good* reason made her get in the car that killed her? The minister just looked at me. I still don't understand. A twenty-year-old girl—one minute, laughing, happy, sweet and kind, and the next, gone.

"I just want you to know what we offer," Elizabeth says. "I'll get you some supplies. And then I'll show you how to empty his catheter."

His catheter.

I forgot I'd be in charge of that.

She walks outside and I watch from the window, rub my jaw. She comes back up the walkway with a cardboard box from her trunk, and I'm waiting for her by the front door.

"I'll visit twice a week, but if you need me, just call."

The box has bandages, gauze, a thermometer, a box of rubber gloves. I stare at the contents, feel more light-headed, put the box on the floor, then sit on the couch.

Elizabeth sits on the couch, too. "We got a lot accomplished today."

"Yeah, we did."

"The hospice doctor will come out one day this week to examine your father."

"A *house call?* That's a new one."

"Hospice really tries to support the family, make it easier for them."

A few minutes later we go down the hall. Elizabeth explains to Dad what we are going to do. He looks embarrassed. She shows me how to put on rubber gloves quickly, then demonstrates how to empty the bag. Actually, it's easier than I thought. I just unplug the bag from a long tube and empty the bag into the toilet. The difficult part is seeing the look on my father's face.

Ten minutes later we are at the front door saying

goodbye. Elizabeth hugs me. "Call me if you need anything. Anytime—even for moral support."

"I will." There is a deep caring in her expression, and I hug her hard for that. "I love you for putting up with me, helping us."

"I love you, too."

Back in the kitchen, I make a turkey sandwich, pour a glass of juice.

"Dad." I stand at the edge of his room, sandwich and juice in my hands.

He rolls over, looks at me, but doesn't say anything.

"Are you hungry? I made you a sandwich."

He shakes his head, turns his gaze to the window again, and my stomach knots. I don't mean to, but a sigh escapes.

He turns back, sits up a little.

"Melinda."

"Yes?"

"I'm sorry I've been so grouchy lately. I hope you know I appreciate what you're doing for me."

"I know, Dad. It's okay."

"I'm just…I'm scared. That's all."

Before I can say anything, he turns, faces the window, and I know he wants the conversation to be over.

In the kitchen, I take a bite of the sandwich. It tastes like paper, so I shove the bread and turkey down the garbage disposal. I watch raindrops fall, study the place where I planted the daffodils.

"Dad."

It's six-thirty in the morning. I'm standing in the doorway of his room. He's in bed, on his side. The pleated window shade is up. Outside, two dark birds are sitting in the tree beyond his window.

He looks at me, but doesn't say anything.

"How do you feel?"

"Okay."

"Did you sleep well?"

"No. I hate this catheter." He looks away, as if he's ashamed.

"I know. I'll do it really fast. You know our bodies are like cars, we need fuel, have exhaust." I go through the steps Elizabeth showed me, try to make him feel comfortable. When I'm finished, I wash my hands, straighten the bathroom a little then go back into his room. He's still in the same position I left him.

"You want breakfast?"

"No."

"You have to eat. You have your pills to take. Elizabeth said you shouldn't take them on an empty stomach."

"I'm not hungry."

When Jennifer left for college, I felt free for the first time in years. Without a child in the house, there were no breakfasts to worry about, no one to nag about eating well.

"Will you just eat a piece of toast and have some juice?"

He closes his eyes, nods.

"Oh, good." A tiny bit of happiness floats in. I walk briskly to the kitchen, pray I can get a piece of toast back to my father before he changes his mind.

Familiar sunrise paints the kitchen. The rain has gone. Each morning when I stand at this window, I'm amazed that the world looks so new, hopeful. In the cool light, I put the teakettle on, mix the only can of orange juice I have in the same blue pitcher I've made juice in since Jenny was a baby. When the whole-wheat bread pops from the toaster, I butter it.

I dig in the bottom cabinet by the stove where I put things I hardly ever use, and I find the bamboo tray. Last year when I was cleaning out cupboards, I almost gave this tray to the Salvation Army, but for some reason I kept it. The kettle whistles. I pour hot water into the Easter mug Jenny gave me, spoon in Folgers instant coffee.

Behind me, I hear David shuffle into the kitchen, wearing his old blue bedroom slippers. He isn't a morning person. Usually when I wake up, I'm happy. Not David. He's quiet, almost grumpy until he's had his coffee and reads some of the newspaper.

"Morning." I whisper the word. He also acts differently when there is company in the house—a little nervous, as if it bothers him that things aren't the way they always are.

Is Dad considered company? At this point, I'm not sure about anything.

"Morning." He pushes the coffeepot button. At night, right before he goes to bed, he always gets the coffeemaker ready.

I pour juice, put the small glass on the tray.

"What are you doing?" David studies the breakfast tray.

"I'm fixing Dad breakfast. He has to take his pills with some food."

"He's not going to come out here to eat?"

"I don't think he will. He's pretty tired. Plus, he doesn't like to walk around with the catheter."

"He should get up, come out to the table, get a little exercise."

For a moment, I feel like we are talking about Jenny. We used to argue about her behavior, what chores she needed to do around the house. David made it clear he wanted her to help me. But, sometimes, it was just easier to do them myself. When David and I argued, Jenny would slam out of the house, walk to her friends. As she got older, she would grab the keys and blast out of the driveway.

"I don't think Dad wants to get up. And Elizabeth said he has to eat before he takes his pills." I gesture to the tray, point to the pills on the white napkin. They look like miniature jellybeans.

"I don't think—" David's voice is louder than before "—it's a good idea for you to wait on him all the time. He can get up, move around. It would be better for him."

I put my index finger to my lips.

"What?" David says, shakes his head.

"You don't want Dad to hear, do you?" I whisper, gesture back to his room.

David goes over to the coffeepot.

"I just think it would be a good idea if your dad gets up. Moves around. That way you don't have to wait on him and he gets some exercise. That's all."

I pick up the tray, feel guilty and put it down. David's pouring coffee. There's that displeased expression—his jaw tight, his mouth in a straight line.

"I want him to eat so he gets better, David," I say in a harsh whisper. "If it means taking a tray back to his room, that's what I'm going to do."

David looks at me with exasperation. "You always do this."

"Do what?" I whisper.

He turns to the coffeepot, pours cream in his coffee, stirs it. I walk over and tap him on the shoulder.

"Do what?" I whisper again, feel thick tension between us.

He faces me. "You always do more than you have to and don't think of yourself, and then when I try to protect you, you get mad at me."

David isn't whispering and this makes me nervous. What if Dad hears us fighting? What if he goes back to Las Cruces and gets sicker? I close my eyes as worry fills my chest.

"Oh, for God's sake, don't start crying."

My throat tightens and I press my hand against my lips, turn back to the tray, pick it up and go to Dad's room.

"Here you go," I say, try to sound upbeat, happy.

Dad's eyes are closed and it takes a moment for him to open them.

"I made you a piece of wheat toast with just a little butter, some juice. That's it. After you eat, you can take your pills and brush your teeth."

He sits up, swings his legs over the side of the bed. I put the tray on his lap.

"Is it okay?"

"Yeah, it's fine, honey." He takes the juice, sips a little, and my heart soars over the anger.

"Want anything else?"

"No thanks."

Behind me, I hear David shuffling down the hall. He stops at the door, coffee cup in hand, looks in. He's all smiles.

"Hey, Stan, you have a good night?"

"Yeah, had a real good night." Dad picks up the toast, takes a bite.

"It's a beautiful day, sun's out. Later you should go outside and get some sun. Might do you some good."

"I'll probably do that."

Dad and David begin talking about David's latest project. I edge past my husband at the door, go back to the kitchen, pour myself a cup of coffee and look out the window to the growing sunshine.

CHAPTER ELEVEN

"I'm Dr. London."

Dad's hospice doctor is standing at our front door.

"Melinda," I say, shake his hand, and motion him into the house. He is a tall, thin man with dark hair, and a serious expression. "My father's in the back bedroom."

Dr. London follows me down the hall. Yesterday, his secretary called and made an appointment for him to examine my father. Dad is lying in bed, on his back. The pleated window shade is down and the room is dim. This morning, I opened it to let the sun in, but Dad must have gotten up and closed the shade.

"Dad, your doctor's here. Dr. London."

He opens his eyes, looks at us. I click on the overhead light and he sits up.

"Hello, Mr. Howard." Dr. London moves to the end of the bed and shakes Dad's hand. "How are you?"

"Fine. Please call me Stanley."

"I'm Christopher London, the Fort Worth Hospice's advising doctor. I'd like to examine you if you don't mind." His voice is calm and kind, and part of me relaxes.

The doctor and I are sitting in the breakfast nook with Dad's medical records in front of us. While he examined Dad, I came into the kitchen and made a half pot of coffee. I was sure he wouldn't want any, but I thought I should offer. After he said goodbye to Dad and came out to the living room, he accepted my offer of coffee.

"Your father's on a lot of medication." He taps the list of pills I wrote out before he got here. There are ten—including pain medication, three times a day. "Is your father eating?"

"A little."

"Loss of appetite is a problem with cancer patients."

"Is there anything I can do to get him to eat?" I press the table with my fingertips, feel nervous.

"There's not a lot. The protocol is offer food, but don't make an issue out of it or force him to eat. If he's hungry, he'll eat."

"No one told me that in Las Cruces." I tried so hard to get my father to eat. Maybe I made the situation worse.

"I know you're worried about your father. We're here to help you. You can call me anytime or call the hospice. We want to be straightforward with answers, help our patients and their families. Do you have any questions?"

I study the table for a moment, then look at the doctor. His expression is so kind, it opens my heart a little.

"How sick is my father?"

He takes a sip of black coffee, puts the mug down and folds his hands.

"He probably has about three months."

Three months! This is not the answer I wanted to hear.

His words wrap around my body and squeeze the breath out of me.

"No one can say for sure," the doctor continues. "Death, like life, is unpredictable. But in cases like these—"

"Death? I wanted to know when he'll get better." I feel weird, as if my head is not attached to my body. I look out the window, try to study the trees, the grass, but everything blurs together. Three months—twelve weeks. How many days and hours is that? I try to calculate it, but I can't.

Dr. London touches my shoulder. "I'm sorry."

My jaw tightens and my lips flatten against each other—I'm closing up like a flower.

"This is never easy. Your father's a nice man. When I was examining him, we talked about jogging."

"He must have liked that." A dull ache begins pulsing inside my chest. "Everybody is different. If anyone can beat this thing, it's my father. Did he tell you how many marathons he's run? How many architectural awards he's received—really prestigious ones?"

"We only talked about running."

"I appreciate your honesty, you coming out here. But I think my father is going to surprise you, surprise everyone."

"Bone cancer from the prostate is usually very aggressive at this stage."

"But you don't know my father. When he puts his mind to something, well, you'll see." I fold my hands, feel resolve building inside me, over the shock, the numbness. "My father is going to get better."

"I hope he does." His expression is sincere.

"How do you do this job? You could be delivering babies. Giving life instead of guessing at how long someone has to live and telling their families," I say, gesture toward my father's room.

Dr. London studies me for a moment, rubs his bottom lip with his index finger.

"My mother died of breast cancer when I was thirteen. I've never forgotten the look on my father's face. She was in and out of hospitals for months at a time. It was hard on her, our family. Our lives were completely changed. Hospice care would have made it easier for my mother, our family."

I nod, think about Vanessa. Months after her death, I sat in the student union laughing and suddenly, from out of nowhere, it hit me, I was having a good time and my friend was gone. I started walking back to the dorm, but in the middle of the campus or somewhere, I can't really remember, I looked up at the dark sky with so many stars and, for the first time, I realized my life would never be the same.

Dr. London reaches down, takes a folder out of his briefcase.

"My office is in Fort Worth." He points to the address at the top of the first page.

I recognize it. Pennsylvania Avenue is in the middle of the hospital district. "I know that area."

"If your father needs anything, please call me." He points to his office number. "The hospice nurse will help, and you can always call the hospice office, but if you need to talk to me, have any questions, don't hesitate to call. Nothing is too small to ask."

I shake my head. "I don't have any more questions." I don't want to ask questions because I don't want to have to fight the answers.

"I'd like to see your father once a week, so if you'll call my office, my receptionist will make an appointment. You have a hospice nurse coming out twice a week?"

I nod. "Elizabeth."

"And the nurse's aide?"

"Yes, three times a week."

"Good." He leans back, looks at Dad's medications again. "He can be taken off most of these."

I study the list, wonder if this is the right thing to do, if it's part of the surrender method hospice uses. "Aren't they helping him?"

"No. The only medication he needs is for pain."

"Are you sure?"

"Yes. Has he complained of pain?"

"No, not since he left the hospital."

"You might even cut back on the pain pills."

I write down what he's said.

He studies me a moment. "I know this is difficult. Do you work outside the home?"

"No. Not right now. I did, though." That part of my life seems so long ago.

"What did you do?"

"I taught English."

He smiles. "Not my best subject."

"Really?" Looking at this man, one would think he'd be good at most anything.

"Math, science were my better subjects. My daughter is having trouble with English. I guess it runs in the family."

"Expect a lot. That's what I always told parents. You could get a tutor for her."

"Good advice. Do you think you'll go back to teaching?" He takes the last sip of his coffee.

"I'm not sure." I gesture to Dad's room. "I want to get my father through this first."

He nods, looks solemn, kind.

"How many children do you have?" I ask.

"One daughter."

"Us, too. Ours is in college."

"My wife and I wanted three, but she can't have any more."

I hear a tiny feather of grief in his voice. "I'm sorry."

"We love kids." He looks out to the front yard. "But sometimes things don't always work out the way we want or wish they would."

I hear his words—*three months*. I nod. "Yes, I know."

I close the front door, shift my attention to the window and watch Dr. London drive away in his plain black sedan.

In my father's room, I see Dad's in the same position he usually is in, hands on his chest with his eyes closed.

"Dad?" I whisper in case he's asleep.

He opens his eyes, and I go to the left side of his bed.

"Yeah?"

"Did you like the doctor?"

"Yeah, he was okay."

"He drove all the way up from Fort Worth to see you."

My father's eyes widen. "He did?"

Oh, God, I shouldn't have said that. I make myself smile, sit on the edge of the bed, and Dad moves over a little to make room for me.

"Yes, he usually makes a house call for the first visit with all his patients." I'm so afraid I will spin my father into more depression by saying the wrong thing that I don't know what to say. Maybe hospice doesn't know what they're doing with all their honesty and straightforwardness.

"Right."

I take his hand, hold it for a moment.

"He said he likes to see his patients every week. It's routine. I can drive to his office with you until you get better. I'll even drive, if you want me to or navigate. Remember when I used to do that?"

Right after my parents divorced, Dad took Lena and me on a trip to Montana. On the way, he taught me how to read a map so I could help him drive through the cities. Then, later, after I was married, he'd call and tell me about his travel plans. I'd get out a map, run my finger along the highways as he spoke about them. He always sounded so excited. Maybe driving to Dr. London's office will help him feel better.

Dad turns a little more on his side, looks at me.

"If I didn't have this bag attached to me, I'd be more comfortable."

I think about the clear plastic tube that is hidden under the covers. It must be so uncomfortable for him.

"I know. But it'll be nice to get out, take a drive once a week. We could stop somewhere for lunch."

"I'm not stopping anywhere with this."

"Then we'll stop at a drive-in. You won't have to go in. You know Texas, we have tons of drive-ins."

He shakes his head. "I'll go down to his office, but no lunch."

"Dad," I say, wait for him to look at me. He opens his eyes slowly and I can tell he was asleep.

"Do you want to eat? Dinner's ready."

"No, thanks, honey. I had enough at lunch."

"You only had a sandwich. Maybe later?"

"Yeah, maybe later."

I walk back to the kitchen, fill David's and my plates. I have cooked a pork roast, rice and tossed a salad. This afternoon, after the doctor left, and Dad and I talked about driving to Fort Worth, he did eat a whole turkey sandwich.

I sit across from David at the dining table. All day

I've been thinking about what Dr. London said, brushing it from my mind like fallen leaves on the grass.

"Dinner looks great," David says.

I push rice around my plate with my fork. "David?"

He looks at me, still chewing. "Yeah?"

"Dad's hospice doctor came out today."

"A house call?" He wrinkles his forehead. "How much do you think that's gonna cost?"

"I don't know." I clasp my hands. "Elizabeth explained the other day that hospice files all the insurance."

"That's good, less paperwork for you."

"He examined Dad, said he wanted to see him every week. I thought next week I'd drive Dad to his office."

The familiar look of worry appears on David's face.

"You have to drive Stan down to Fort Worth every week?"

"Maybe not every week, just until he feels better. It'll be good for Dad to get out, you know? And I don't mind going with him."

"I feel bad you have to do all this."

"I need to get out of the house, too. You want to know what else Dr. London told me?" I need to explain to someone that the doctor is wrong, that the medical profession is crazy.

"Of course." David puts down his fork.

"He said Dad probably only has three months."

He blinks as if he's trying to understand what I've just said. Then, suddenly, as the meaning of my words sink in, his expression crumbles a little.

"He said that?"

"Yes. But I think he's wrong. Doctors don't know everything. I mean, they even call what they do a practice." I study my clasped hands, swallow over the lump that has suddenly developed in my throat.

"Hell, people get misdiagnosed all the time," he says, picks up his fork, but doesn't eat anything.

I nod, stand, look at my full plate. "I'm going to go back and help Dad get ready for bed."

"I'm worried about you. You're doing too much." David glances back to Dad's room. "You spend a lot of time in there when I'm home. I know you must spend more during the day."

"Dad needs the help right now. He's going to beat this, and then he can go home, be fine."

"Yeah." David gets up, pats my shoulder, stands

beside me as if he's waiting for me to say something else. When I don't, he walks over and clicks on the TV. A news report about home invasion blares through the room and we listen. The reporter explains that someone broke into a house only six blocks away.

"I think I'll put the house alarm on tonight before we go to bed," David says.

"That's probably a good idea."

I walk down the hall toward my father's room. I'm tired, feel hollow inside, like one of those big chocolate Easter bunnies that looks so heavy, yet when it's cracked open, it's empty.

CHAPTER TWELVE

The blare from the house alarm wakes me. I sit up. David must have forgotten that the house alarm was on and opened the bathroom window.

Dad!

I bolt out of bed, run down the hall into his bedroom. My father is standing in his wrinkled blue pajamas trying to open the window across from his bed.

"Dad, it's okay."

He looks at me with terror. "What's happening?"

"It's just the house alarm. It's okay." I rush to him, put my arm around his shoulders. He's trembling and this breaks my heart. "David forgot to turn it off before he opened the bathroom window. That's all."

The intense sound stops and the silence is good.

"It's okay. See, it's gone." I guide him back to bed, but my ears are still ringing and I imagine how Dad must have felt—startled, then scared.

David walks into Dad's room, looks around. "I'm

sorry, I forgot the alarm was on when I opened the bathroom window."

Dad doesn't say anything. He's sitting on the edge of the bed, his head down, his hands between his legs. The end of his catheter is hanging free.

Oh, God!

The tubing probably got caught in the covers when he bolted out of bed and it pulled out.

"Dad, are you okay?" I put my hand on his shoulder. He's still trembling, but he nods. "Your catheter came out."

He glances at the plastic tubing and his expression turns to disbelief.

"I heard the alarm. I thought something terrible was happening and I wanted to get out of here."

"It's okay." But I don't know if he's all right. I check the floor, the sheets. There's no blood. "You aren't in pain?"

He shakes his head.

David looks at me. "I forgot the alarm was on. What should we do?"

"I'll call Elizabeth. She'll know what to do."

We are in the Fort Worth hospital waiting room. Dad is slumped in one of the stiff hospital chairs, staring at the floor. David is sitting one chair over from him, reading a magazine and I'm sitting in the middle.

Elizabeth told me, since it's Saturday, I needed to take Dad to the emergency room to have a new catheter inserted.

When I explained this to David, he offered to drive us, I guess because he felt guilty. Dad didn't say anything. I asked him a few times if he was in pain and he just shook his head.

The waiting room isn't as busy as I expected. The woman at the desk told me it would only be about a twenty-minute wait because she has to get the urologist, who's on call, to come in.

I pat my father's shoulder. "It'll be okay. They'll fix you up."

He sits up, leans closer. "I don't like being a bother."

"You aren't a *bother*, don't be silly. Accidents happen every day. Besides, it wasn't your fault. David opened the window. We'll blame it on him." I force a laugh. "Maybe not these kinds of accidents happen every day, but we didn't have anything else to do today."

The woman at the desk stands up, calls Dad's name.

"That's you." I gently nudge him with my shoulder. He stands and so do I. "It's going to be okay, you'll see." I hug him. "We'll be out of here in no time and then we'll have the entire afternoon to relax."

He doesn't say anything, heads down the hall behind the receptionist. I sit down next to David, lean against him.

"I feel bad." The rumble of my husband's voice is so familiar. "I'm an idiot for setting off the alarm."

"No, you aren't. It was an honest mistake. I just hate that you have to waste your Saturday in a hospital waiting room."

"Don't worry about it."

At times, I know David so well. We met at the University of Texas twenty-four years ago. David was a senior and I was a sophomore. His friend Jack Amber was taking the same Psychology One class I was. Jack was and still is a lax guy. That year he had to retake the class because he'd flunked it the semester before.

On the first day, after the professor dismissed us, Jack asked me to share my notes with him because he was planning on missing every Tuesday for baseball practice. I stammered I would, didn't know what else to say. So on Fridays, Jack would find me in the student union and I'd give him a copy of my notes.

One Friday, David came with him, and after Jack left, with notes in hand, David and I talked for a little while, then he suggested we have dinner.

That day I thought he was clean-cut with his short brown hair, his tall, muscled body—an older man. I was really shy in those days and I could barely say yes to the date. David picked me up on time at my dorm. He looked perfect in his beige dress slacks and white knit shirt. We went to dinner at a local pizza parlor by the college, then walked the campus. He talked about architecture. I loved listening—he's always been so enthusiastic about his work. But most of all, he seemed to need someone to listen.

At eleven-thirty, he brought me back to the dorm, explained that I shouldn't be so nice to Jack. I asked him what he meant by that and he said I was the kind of person people always took advantage of. Then he kissed me on the cheek and left.

We went out three times before he kissed me on the lips—my first real kiss. I tried to pretend it wasn't, but David knew and he told me so, said he was happy he was the first man I'd kissed. Two years later, after I graduated, we were married. He was already in Fort Worth, at the firm he's with now. When he was at the university, he'd won awards for his designs, and as soon as he graduated, the firm snapped him up, and after our three-day honeymoon to Oklahoma, I began teaching.

"You okay?" David asks now.

"Yeah. I was just thinking about you."

"Are you mad about the alarm?"

"No, of course not. It was an accident."

"Good."

A tall man, about our age, walks into the hospital waiting room and the woman at the counter directs him to us. I stand and so does David.

"I'm Dr. Johnson. Your father is okay. There's no damage. He told me the reason he had the catheter was because of scar tissue and his bladder shut down?"

"That's what the doctor in Las Cruces said."

"I examined him and I didn't see any scar tissue. He seems hydrated. I don't think the catheter is needed anymore."

I look at the doctor in disbelief. "He doesn't need the catheter? Why would they put it in if he doesn't need it?"

"I don't think he needs it now," he says, but doesn't really answer my question. "If you're willing to bring him back to the hospital if he can't urinate on his own, I think we should leave it out."

A tiny kernel of hope expands through my chest. "I'll bring him back if we need to. I'll do anything."

"Bring him back to this hospital? You mean, all the way back here?" David asks, and I want to kick him.

"It's no problem, really. I'll bring him back if I have to. Honest." I feel panicky that the doctor might change his mind. I turn to David. "You don't have to come with us. Maybe we won't have to come back at all."

"I think he'll be able to urinate on his own, but there's a slight possibility he can't."

I rub my forehead, think back to Las Cruces. That seems so long ago. What other mistakes could they have made?

"I'll bring him back if he can't pee, I promise. How long should we wait?"

"He drank some water a few minutes ago. He should urinate in three or four hours. No later. If he doesn't, then he'll need to come back. It could turn into a dangerous situation."

I let the hope that's fluttering in my chest free. It roams around my body, warms my muscles, makes me smile.

"I'll bring him back. That's no problem. I'm sure Dad would like to try this."

We are on our way home. I'm sitting in the front and Dad is in the back, staring out the window. I turn a little, reach over and touch his knee. When he looks at me I smile and he smiles back. He seems happy.

"Hey, Stan, you feeling the urge to go?" David glances in the rearview mirror then laughs. "The pressure's on, you know?"

"Yeah, the pressure's on." Dad chuckles.

As we pulled onto the freeway, I crossed my fingers in hope that my father can pee when he gets home. David begins talking about a basketball game he's planning to watch this afternoon.

"Stan, you should watch the game with me."

"Might do that. Just might do that."

The winter sky travels along with us as we head down the long strip of highway. Texas skies are beautiful, even when there are rain clouds. Today it seems as though someone painted this sky, it's so perfect with the daubing of clouds, the pretty blue.

"Please let him pee," I say under my breath, knowing that this could be a turning point for him.

"What?" David asks.

I turn, smile. "Nothing."

As soon as we get home, Dad goes back to his bathroom. I sit at the breakfast nook table with my hands clinched white.

"I hope he can pee," I whisper for the hundredth time. In the car about halfway home, I added *Dear God*, but that felt so uncomfortable, I didn't say the two words again. When we were kids, my parents took Lena and me to church, but our trips were sporadic, self-imposed journeys to raise moral children. So I'm not really sure how to pray and I don't believe in it anyway. But today, for some reason, I felt it might help.

"Melinda."

Dad is standing at the edge of the breakfast nook smiling.

"Did you?"

"Yeah. Isn't that great?" He smiles broadly.

I get up, wrap my arms around him, feel elated.

I haven't been so happy about pee since I potty trained Jennifer.

"Oh, Dad, I'm so glad. What wonderful news."

"Yeah." He hugs me again. "I think I'll watch the basketball game with David."

It's been three days since we had to take my father to the emergency room. The next morning, I walked into the kitchen and found Dad standing in front of the sink, looking out the window. This was the first time he'd come out into the kitchen since he's been here.

The sunrise painted the room and Dad with a stunning pink. I stayed for a moment at the edge of the kitchen and watched him. He gazed out the window, his fingers rubbing the countertop, the back of his head looking so perfect.

"Dad," I finally said.

He turned around and his expression was a study in wonder. He gestured to the world outside. "You know, life is really beautiful."

I went over to the window, stood next to him. More light flooded the room, us, the yard, like when we were in the New Mexico church.

"It is, isn't it?"

"I'd forgotten how really wonderful life is."

"Most mornings I come out here and take a few minutes to enjoy it."

"You're a smart girl." He stared at me for a moment. "I was just thinking how much I've missed not paying attention to the important parts of life—people, the world around me."

Then he touched my shoulder for a brief moment and I could see tears in his eyes.

My whole body felt alive with happiness that morning. We stood for another moment by the window and looked in amazement at the trees, the flowers, all showered in fresh pink light.

Now I spoon oatmeal into a bowl for Dad, sprinkle cinnamon over the top like I used to do for Jenny, take it over to the table and sit across from my father.

"How are you feeling?" I ask.

"Aren't you going to eat?"

I shake my head. "I'm not hungry, I'll eat later. You feel better, don't you?"

"Yeah, I do." He eats a spoonful of oatmeal, looks out to the yard. "I couldn't stand that catheter. It made me feel sick, depressed, as if I were chained to my illness. I just wanted to lie in bed."

"I understand that."

Dad continues eating and I focus my attention on the yard.

"I planted the daffodil bulbs you sent me for my birthday around that tree." I point to the area where they are. "I can't wait for them to come up. Elizabeth said they'll be beautiful. I'm glad you bought them for me."

He nods, swallows. "When I saw them, for some reason I thought of you, thought you'd like them. I can't wait, either. I'm sure they'll be nice."

I study the sunlight for a long moment, think about what Dr. London said. Doctors are wrong all the time—like with the catheter. Things change, turn into better circumstances.

"Don't you think it's weird about the alarm?" I ask. "Last night I realized if David hadn't set off the alarm we never would have known you didn't need the catheter."

Earlier when I made this observation to David he laughed, said it was just a coincidence. Before I would have agreed. I don't believe in fate or anything like that. To me, life is a random mess, a swirling chaos of events. But when I think of what happened the other day, it just seems so odd that David would turn on the TV at the exact moment when they were talking about home invasions.

Dad swallows another spoonful of oatmeal. In the last three days, he's eating more. This morning, I was actually excited about cooking breakfast.

"It's like the whole alarm thing was meant to be," I say.

"I've always believed there's a plan. That someone up there is taking care of us. What about you?"

"I don't have any beliefs, Dad. Not since my friend in college died."

"You don't?" He seems surprised at this information.

I nod. "After Vanessa, I just kind of stopped believing, not that I had many beliefs before. I couldn't stop wondering why something like that could happen. I never understood it."

He studies the yard, then turns back. "Life's pretty much a mystery with its beauty, but then tough times hit."

"Yeah, it is."

He reaches over and touches my hand. "I'm sorry about your friend. Did I ever say that?"

I shake my head, not sure my father even knew about Vanessa's accident.

"I don't think so, but you were working. Mom came to be with me for the weekend, went with me to the funeral."

"I was always working." He sighs. "Trying to make buildings perfect." He glances out to the yard again. "Life doesn't have to be perfect, does it? Nature is so beautiful on its own."

"Maybe our flaws are beautiful, too." I think about this, hope it's true, feel good that we're talking. We sit quietly while Dad eats. When he's finished, he stands.

"I'm better without that darned catheter. I was thinking maybe I'd get dressed and walk around the backyard. Would that be okay?"

It's odd that he's asking my permission. "Of course. It's supposed to be warm today. We could walk around the block if you want."

"No, I want to stay by the house in case something happens. I could fall. If I'm in the backyard, I'll be close. I really miss exercising."

"I know you do."

We both stare at the yard and, suddenly, it turns bright with sunlight.

CHAPTER THIRTEEN

First Week in February

It's seven o'clock. I'm standing in Dad's room. He's lying on his bed, still dressed in jeans, reading the *Newsweek* I bought him this afternoon at the grocery store.

"You doing okay?"

He looks up, smiles. "I'm fine, honey."

I go by the bed. He moves over a little and I sit next to him.

"David's still not home. It must be a long meeting."

"I've been through those. He'll be home soon. He's just trying to make the project better, fix all the mistakes."

"Dad, are you angry about the catheter?" In the past four days, I've wondered so many times how a mistake like that could be made—my father having to deal with a catheter when it wasn't even needed.

"I'm a little mad. But I'm happy Dr. Johnson found out I don't need it."

"Well, I'm angry. What if the alarm hadn't gone off? We never would have known."

Dad shrugs. "I know, but I'm beginning to realize that mistakes are part of life. And if you try to make life perfect, it can get miserable."

"I guess." I turn a little. "Did you know you walked twenty minutes today?"

This morning, Dad walked slowly around our backyard. He walks differently now, bends his arm at a funny angle, leans forward. David thinks he's compensating because he's gotten so thin. I'm not sure what it is.

I sat in the family room with my coffee and watched him. Each time he passed the window, I whispered, "Go, Dad." When he finished, I was so excited, I called David. The same excitement filled my body when Jennifer took her first steps. That day, she and I were in the living room of our tiny Fort Worth apartment. I held her hands as she lifted her feet high—pranced like a pony—and suddenly I knew I could let go.

Jenny took five quick steps, then stopped and stared at me with baby surprise. She took three more steps and sat down. I picked her up, danced her around the room, and two days later, she was walking!

Yesterday, Elizabeth said Dad's progress is a miracle. Even David is amazed at the change. I want to believe this, block out what Dr. London said. But I still have this odd feeling. It is so tiny that I sometimes forget it's there, in my chest, right by my heart. Most days, I manage to cover it with positive thoughts, make it lie still, but every once in a while, when I look at Dad, the worry spreads across my body like an amoeba and I have to take a deep breath.

I just hung up the phone.

A moment ago, David, Dad and I were watching "Wheel of Fortune" in the family room. They always get the puzzle before I do, so when the phone rang, I didn't mind being interrupted. I got up, thought the call might be from my sister Lena.

I walk back into the family room. David mutes the Sunny Delight commercial blaring through the room.

"Who was that?" he asks.

I smile more, turn my head a little. "It was Rebecca Mills from the school district."

"And?" David asks.

Dad is staring at me. I smile at him and he smiles back.

"She offered me a *job*."

"Thought you didn't want to go back to teaching junior high."

"I don't. That's not the job. This one is teaching an adult education course, English as a Second Language, on Tuesday and Thursday nights, for two hours."

"That's great, honey," Dad says, sits up a little more. "Really great. You'd be good at that."

"You want to go back to work now?" David leans forward.

"Rebecca said the job would be perfect for me. It's part-time." She was the principal of the junior high school where I taught, but now she works for school administration. We always got along well and, when I quit, she begged me not to.

"How much does it pay?" David shifts in his chair, looks at the TV. "Wheel of Fortune" is back on.

"I don't know. I forgot to ask." I look at Dad, make my eyes big. He gives me a thumbs-up.

"How can you take a job when you don't even know how much it pays?" David asks.

"Well, I didn't think about the money. I was so excited that someone actually wanted me to work at something other than teaching junior high. It probably doesn't pay much, but it would be good for my résumé. And I could find out if I like it."

"Where is it?"

"At Heritage High School. Rebecca's going to bring the textbook over tomorrow. I start in a couple of days."

With the job offer, I realize I miss working more than I thought. Having contact with people, making money of my own was good.

David shakes his head. "I don't like you out at night, by yourself."

I glance at Dad. He's watching the muted "Wheel of Fortune" and I'm embarrassed that David and I are bickering in front of him.

"It's only for two hours, two nights a week," I say.

"Sounds like you've already made up your mind."

David turns the TV sound back on, gets up and goes into the kitchen. I follow him, find him at the sink, filling a water glass.

"You really don't care if I take the job, do you?" I whisper so my father won't hear.

"If it will make you happy, take it."

"You seem a little pissed off."

"I'm not, but what about your father?" He

motions toward the family room, then takes a sip of water, puts the glass down.

"He's doing better. I don't need to be here after dinner. That's when he watches TV. Then right after, he goes back to bed."

"Do you think it's going to stay like this? What did that hospice doctor tell you?"

I think about Dr. London's prediction and my body goes a little numb. I stare at the floor for a moment to center myself. I really want this job.

"Dad's doing better. Elizabeth calls it a *miracle*."

"Melinda, I was thinking today that we have to be realistic."

"I want to. Like we said, doctors don't know everything. That's realistic. Look at the mistakes they made in Las Cruces. I believe Dad's going to get better. He seems better."

Neither of us says anything for a moment.

"We need to keep thinking positively, David."

"Okay. What about the job?"

"Rebecca told me the students are usually Hispanic adults. There won't be any discipline problems and I can be really creative with the lessons. She said if I don't teach the class, they'll have to cancel it."

David drinks more water.

I walk to the sink, try to look out to the trees, the pansies, but all I see is our reflection.

"I'm driving Dad to the doctor's tomorrow."

My husband drinks the rest of the water. "That's good." He cups my shoulder. "And I'm happy about your job." He puts the glass on the counter beside me and walks out of the kitchen.

Dad and I are sitting in Dr. London's waiting room. I'm excited because I can't wait to see what the doctor says about Dad's progress—how much better he is. Deep down, I want to say, *I told you so*, but, of course I won't.

I look over at my father. He's wearing a plaid shirt, jeans, and his skin color is good. He grins and I smile back.

"Dr. London is going to be surprised at your progress."

"Yeah, I think he is."

I pick up a magazine and thumb through the pages. A moment later the receptionist calls Dad back. He stands, walks through the door to one of the exam rooms.

I begin reading an article about spring house-cleaning, realize I need to reorganize closets next week. Twenty minutes later the receptionist ushers me into Dr. London's office. He's sitting at his desk. I take the chair in front of it.

"Your father's doing much better."

I nod, look around. "Where's Dad?"

"He's getting dressed."

"His hospice nurse calls his progress a miracle."

He leans forward. "You're with him most of the time. What do *you* think it is?"

"Well, I'm not one to believes in miracles. I think the catheter was making Dad depressed, he even said he hated it. And all those pills weren't helping. Did he tell you what happened with the catheter?"

"Not the best way to remove it, but there was no damage. I received a letter from Dr. Johnson."

"Coincidence, I think not," I say, then feel like an idiot. Vanessa and I used that expression when we'd studied really hard and passed an exam or did well in a class. "I mean…the accident was like it was meant to be. You know what I mean?" I stop, feel like I'm babbling.

"You mean fate?"

"Yes. If my husband hadn't turned on the news, if our house alarm hadn't gone off, then we might never have known Dad didn't need the catheter. Honestly, we never turn the alarm on. It was just a coincidence that happened."

Dr. London nods. "I would have sent him to a urologist in a few weeks."

"So you don't think it's a miracle?" I really would like to know how all this could have happened, how the events seem to fit together so perfectly.

"I was taught in medical school to believe in science. To find an explanation for everything," he says.

"Is there one for this? The way everything fit together. How much better my father is?"

"Mistakes were made. So if I think about it in that context, then it was a mistake that was found out. Your father said he's eating more?"

"Yeah, three small meals a day, but that's so much better, too. Maybe it *is* a miracle," I say, then laugh. "I have no idea, but I'm glad it happened."

He smiles.

"Did Dad tell you I have a job?" I ask, then realize my father wouldn't tell his doctor this. And why would Dr. London care? But I feel so happy about life right now—how much better my father is—it's difficult to contain myself.

To my surprise his eyes light up. "A job. You do? That's great. Teaching?"

"Teaching English to adults. I start tomorrow night. I can still help Dad, but since he's more mobile, he doesn't need me as much now."

"Teaching English as a Second Language would be very rewarding."

"I've never done it, but I like to help people."

"So do I."

I look to the door that leads to the exam rooms, wonder where my father is. I turn back around.

"I was thinking Dad might be able to go home in a few weeks."

"You have to remember your father still has cancer."

I press my lips together. *Mistakes were made.*

"He's probably in remission," Dr. London says. "But the disease is very unpredictable."

"Right. I understand." I know doctors have to stay reserved in their diagnoses, can't give people hope too soon. "But he's so much better."

"Yes, he is."

"Did you tell Dad he might be in remission? He doesn't talk about the cancer, and I don't bring it up." I shift, cross my arms. "I was just wondering."

"I told him whatever he's doing, he needs to keep on doing it. He didn't ask any questions, doesn't seem to want to know. We talked about jogging and his walking. But if he asks you, I would tell him the truth."

CHAPTER FOURTEEN

I'm standing in my new classroom at Heritage High School. The fluorescent lights are flickering, making the room seem a little unreal. It's a typical room, with desks, bulletin boards, posters, student essays and two whiteboards. The teacher who uses it in the daytime must teach history.

Rebecca brought me my textbook yesterday afternoon, after we got back from Dr. London's office. I read the first chapter of *Circle of Words*. I'm still not sure how to teach this course. And I'm nervous that I don't speak Spanish. I explained this to her, and Rebecca told me not to worry. She reminded me everything doesn't have to be perfect, like I tried to make it when I was teaching junior high. I just need to show up and talk with my students.

I fan myself with the paper I'm going to use to list students' names and phone numbers, in case I ever have to cancel a class. I pulled seven desks into a circle—that's how many students signed up.

I sit in the desk that faces the door, reach down, dig through my briefcase and find the textbook. First, I'm going to talk to each student so I can determine how much English he or she knows. Then I hope we can do the first exercises in the book.

The door opens and two women walk in. They are the same height—small, dark-haired, in their early forties. They see me and stop.

"Hello. I'm Melinda, your instructor." I stand, extend my hand.

They do the same and we shake hands. They are Lulu and Lupé. I gesture to the desks. "Please sit, make yourselves comfortable."

We find our chairs, smile at each other and a nervousness flutters inside me. Another woman rushes in. She's older, heavier, with long dark hair past her shoulders. When she smiles, I see she's missing a tooth on the lower left side of her mouth. The three women talk in Spanish for a few moments, then look at me. It's obvious they know each other.

"What's your name?" I ask the older woman.

"Sue."

Again they talk in Spanish, laugh. I wait for a moment, then hold up my hand.

"English only, please." The room goes silent as they nod, and my face begins to ache from smiling so much.

"We'll wait for the others." I thumb through the textbook, feel badly for stopping their conversation.

It is ten after seven. Dad and David are either watching the "O'Reilly Factor" or Dad has gone back to his room. I feel a little like I did when Jenny was small and I'd leave her with the babysitter or David. I'd always worry, wonder if she was okay. Then I'd go home and everything was fine.

I look at the students.

"I'm Melinda, your instructor," I say, pointing to myself, feel idiotic because I've said this before. And who else would I be?

They smile, nod.

"Your name is?" I ask again, pointing to the woman directly across from me. I think she's the youngest, and appears to know more English.

"Lulu."

I continue around the circle. The other women say their names and then there's another long silence. I shuffle through the papers I brought, find my lesson plan. My plan was to ask questions and figure out where I should start from the students' answers. I take a deep breath, look at the empty desks. I guess no one else is coming.

"Let's move the desks closer." I motion with my hands. The women look at me, but don't do anything. I stand, push an empty desk back into the row I got it from. Soon we are sitting in a small, four-desk circle.

"Lupé, how are you?" I pronounce each word carefully.

She looks at me, smiles, nods her head. It's obvious she doesn't understand.

"She fine," Lulu says and giggles nervously.

"And how are you?"

"Fine."

"Are you happy?"

"Jes, happy."

Lupé and Sue look at Lulu, their eyes wide, then they turn back to me and nod.

"Sue, how are you?"

She grins. The gap in her teeth makes her appear childlike. As if she realizes I can see the space, she brings her hand to her lips, hides behind it.

Lulu says something to Sue in Spanish that sounds like a reprimand.

"I fine." Sue mumbles the two words with a heavy accent.

"I'm fine, too," I say, still feel nervous.

"You are fine?" Lulu asks, motioning with her hand.

I look at them. They seem so eager to learn, so glad to be here.

"You are fine," Lupé and Sue say together, then giggle.

I laugh, wonder if they, too, have worries hidden behind their pretty dark eyes. Maybe they're concerned their teacher doesn't know what the hell she's doing. If so, they're right.

"Hey, I'm home," I say as I walk into the family room that is pewter with the light from the TV. And David seems as if he's suspended in his chair. "How's Dad?"

"He's great. He watched TV for a little while, then went back to his room. How was the teaching?"

The clock on the mantel reads nine. I let class out early because I ran out of material. The women didn't seem to mind. They chatted with each other as we walked from the school. In the parking lot, cold wind blew our hair, nudged us along. Then we shook hands and I told them I'd see them Tuesday. Lulu spoke for everyone, said they'd be back, thanked me, then we all ran for our cars with the wind at our backs.

"It's a small class, but I think it's better that way." I don't want to tell David that I felt uncomfortable and over half the class didn't show up.

"That's good. I'm glad you're home."

I go into the kitchen, uncork the already-opened Robert Mondavi Chardonnay, pour some into a good wineglass. The cold feels good against my warm skin. As I walk down the hall the canned laughter from the TV reaches me, follows me. Dad's light is off, but the night-light in the bathroom illuminates his bedroom. He's lying on the bed, staring at the ceiling.

"Hey, Dad," I whisper.

"Hi, honey." His gaze shifts to me and he sits up a little.

I cross the room, stand by his bed. He pats the bedspread and moves over. I sit on the edge, feel comfort in the semidarkness.

"How was your class?"

"Okay. But only three people came. Three women."

"Three's better than none."

"I guess. But I don't know what I'm doing. I've never taught English like this. I felt a little inadequate." I wonder if the women will come back, if I'll even have a class next week.

"You probably did better than you think. You're a good teacher, and you know more English than they do."

"But I feel bad."

He sits up a little more. "Why?"

"I don't know, I guess I expected a full class, wanted it perfect."

"With less students you can get more accomplished."

"True."

"It'll work out the way it's supposed to. Most things do."

"You think so?" I look at him through the dim light, still feel tension in my forehead, shoulders.

"Yeah, I didn't think that when I was your age, but I believe it now. Wait and see. You like teaching and you're a nice person. That's all that counts."

I've always felt comfortable teaching, even when I was at the junior high school and wanted to quit. The first time I walked into a classroom, it was as if

I'd been there forever. But with junior high, I think I just got tired, maybe even bored doing the same thing for so long.

"Your students want to learn English," Dad says. "That's all you need to keep in mind. And you're good at that. Plus, they'll learn you care about them. Every person needs someone who cares. If you have that, even if life isn't perfect, it isn't so bad."

"I guess you're right." I take a sip of wine, hold out the glass to him. "Want some? It's a Robert Mondavi Chardonnay."

He shakes his head. "I'd better not. I feel pretty tired tonight."

"I'll get you your own glass."

He laughs. "No, I'm not sure wine would sit well with me tonight. Seems I'm always tired."

"I'm sorry."

"Maybe because I walked a lot today. Must have worn myself out."

I press my lips together, try not to think about anything else. "Yeah, just don't walk so much tomorrow. You're doing great."

But Dad not wanting any wine reminds me how much his life has changed.

"Remember that story you told me about those rich people and the wine?" I ask.

He looks at me, and even in the faded light, I know he doesn't remember.

"You and Herb Clipman went to dinner with some wealthy clients, and they were being so serious about the wine selection, wanted the perfect one for dinner. Then, when the wine was poured, Herb gargled his as a joke."

Dad laughs. "Oh, yeah. You should have seen their faces. I thought old Herb was going to blow the contract. We were just starting out and needed the money. You know, they ended up giving us a bigger deal. And it worked out better than we expected. Lately I've been thinking and I've figured out most things work out. We worry for nothing, waste a lot of energy trying to fix things when they're okay the way they are."

He sits up a little more. "That's why, don't be so hard on yourself about school, other things, honey. Life always turns out better than we expect."

I take another sip of wine. My body begins to relax a little.

"You really think so?" This feels so good—talking to my father.

"I really do. Did you like the students?"

"Oh, yes. They're nice, very happy."

"Just remember, whatever happens, it's for the best." He leans back a little, sighs and closes his eyes.

I take another sip of wine and pat his hand and wonder if he's right.

Our bedroom is dark except for the moonlight that is glowing through the pleated shades. I sit up a little, look at the alarm clock. I've been asleep for three hours. I get out of bed, walk quietly into the bathroom, close the door and sit on the edge of the bathtub. I should be groggy with sleep, but I'm wide awake.

My hands feel cool against my face. I think about the dream that woke me—can still see Dr. London's anguished expression. In my dream, he and I were sitting on the couch in the living room. He looked so sad, I leaned over and kissed his cheek, tried to comfort him.

I rub my face. The dream felt so real—like the one I had before Jennifer was born.

In the bedroom, David is lying on his side, snoring lightly. I cross the bedroom, walk down the hall to the front door. The cold night air stings my exposed skin. I think about the dream—touchable-real—and I know the memory won't go away.

The concrete porch numbs my bare feet. The yard, the street and sky look as if they've been painted with moonlight. I cross my arms, know what the dream means, yet I push the thought away. Instead, I let myself be mesmerized by the beautiful night.

I'm waiting for Elizabeth, who is fifteen minutes late. I go into the breakfast nook, sit at the table and open *Circle of Words* to the second chapter. The house is so quiet. Dad has already had his oatmeal and orange juice. Now, he's back in his room, brushing his teeth and getting ready to walk around the backyard. David left a few minutes ago.

The sun splashes winter light through the windows. All morning I've tried to brush last night's dream away, but it won't leave. Dr. London's expression haunts me. I wish Elizabeth would get here, so I'd have a distraction. She's been coming to the house once a week since Dad began doing better.

A car door slams. Elizabeth walks around to the other side of her car, gets her bag. I go outside and head down the small sidewalk.

"Hi," I say. She hugs me.

In the kitchen, we stand at the counter. "You want something to drink?"

"No thanks, I just had coffee. Sorry I'm late. I got a call from another patient and then I had to touch base with her doctor. Your dad's my first visit."

"How many visits today?" I imagine her patients, wonder who they are—maybe they have daughters like me, fighting dreams.

"Seven, then I have to go to the office and do some paperwork." She puts her bag on the kitchen counter, faces me. "How's your father doing?"

"He's fine. He's waiting for you and then he'll walk in the backyard."

"I swear it's a miracle. He's doing so much better—really living again. Did he go to his doctor's appointment this week?"

"Yeah, I drove him, but he could drive himself. You know, I don't understand," I whisper this. "First, the doctor said Dad only had three months, then he's sure Dad's in remission."

Elizabeth studies me, turns her head a little as if she's thinking about what to say.

"The doctor's probably right, Melinda, on both parts. Sometimes the cancer quits growing for a while, but then it starts again. The radiation treatments probably helped."

"But Dad's doing so well. I mean, you even said it's a miracle. I don't believe in them, but, I mean, Dad is so much better."

"Sometimes—"

"We had such a good talk last night. I just know he's going to be okay." I take a deep breath and the dream wanders in, wraps itself around me.

"He might be…I just don't want you to get your hopes up. I've seen a lot of patients do this—they have good days, bad days, good weeks, bad weeks. It's nice you're spending time with your father."

I nod, think about last night, how nice it was that Dad and I could talk.

"Did Dr. London say anything else?" Elizabeth asks.

I shake my head. The dream surfaces again and sad feelings overwhelm me.

"What?" Elizabeth asks.

"Do you know Dr. London very well?" I ask.

"He's the best doctor on the hospice staff. Always upbeat, happy. Every nurse wants to work with him because he's so positive. And he never yells."

"Doctors yell?"

"Oh, yeah, some of them yell a lot. But with Dr. London, if I think something needs to be changed with a patient, I don't hesitant to call him. Some doctors don't like being questioned, and they give the nurses a hard time."

I shake my head, amazed at this insight into the medical profession.

"Dr. London was the only doctor who came to the hospice Christmas party last year. And he brought his wife."

"What's she like?" I imagine a pretty woman.

"She's very nice, but very plain, short, stocky, no makeup, long dark hair, kind of like a sixties flower child."

Elizabeth's description reminds me of a girl in college who dressed in black from head to toe and wore her long hair covering half her face. She never spoke to anyone. Vanessa and I were fascinated with her because she was so enigmatic.

"She's mysterious?"

"No. Very nice, open."

"Last night I dreamed about him."

"Who?"

"Dr. London."

"Well, I can understand that. He's a big part of

your father's life right now. The mind has a funny way of processing our emotions."

"In my dream, he looked worried, so sad. I kissed him on the cheek to make him feel better. It was like I was trying to comfort him. Isn't that weird?"

Before Elizabeth can say anything, Dad walks into the kitchen. He's dressed in his usual jeans and plaid shirt. I only brought three changes of clothes so his wardrobe is limited, but he doesn't seem to care. Before, he was so picky about his clothes. He always wore beautiful suits, really neat casual clothes.

"Hi, Elizabeth," he says, smiles.

"Mr. Howard. You look so good!"

"I feel okay. Yesterday, I was a little tired. But today's a better day. I'm going to walk this morning. I'm trying to build up my strength. Just waiting for you."

"Great, we'll take your blood pressure and make some notes. Then you can get to it. I swear you're a walking miracle."

CHAPTER FIFTEEN

Dad felt good enough to come to the English class with me tonight. David had a late meeting, and this afternoon I asked Dad if he wanted to join me. To my surprise, he said yes.

"I thought we'd work on exercises together for the first half of the class, and then we can break into groups. Would you be comfortable working with Lupé and Sue, Dad?"

"Sure." He looks out the car window toward the high school.

"Great, while you're doing that I can help Lulu with her pronunciation."

"That's fine." He nods, looks serious.

We climb out of the car, go to the classroom. The three women are already seated in the desks that they have brought into a circle. I introduce my father and the women stand, shake his hand. Lulu pulls another desk into the circle and my father smiles.

Is this how he looked when he was volunteering at the elementary school? At the end of the school year, Dad went to Kmart and bought pens for the kids with four different colors of ink. He sounded so happy that day when he called me and explained how the students crowded around him, were so excited to get the pens.

Dad and I sit and we begin practicing conversations with the women. An hour later, we're finished.

"Let's break into two groups," I say.

The three women nod, but I don't think they understand the word *groups*. I motion for Sue and Lupé to stay with Dad. I stand and gesture to Lulu to come with me into the hall.

"Dad, will you go over the pictures?" I hand him the stack I clipped out of magazines this afternoon. "Then you can work on vocabulary for restaurant visits, if you want."

"I'll do that." He smiles at Lupé and Sue.

The teacher's manual suggests that the students pretend they are ordering food, and I thought this would be good for them to learn. I open the classroom door for Lulu and we go into the hall, sit in the two chairs by the door. Lulu looks worried. I touch her shoulder, in an effort to make her feel more comfortable.

"Since my father is here—" I gesture back to the classroom "—I thought I'd work with you. Is that okay?"

Her expression relaxes. "Okay."

"We can talk, and then I'll know where you need the most help."

"Okay."

"Do you have children?" I ask.

"Kids?"

"Yes, kids, children?"

"Oh, jes. Three." She holds up three fingers. I love her accent. It's soft and rounds each word.

"Are they girls?"

"Jes, girls, boy."

"I have two girls and one boy," I say slowly, gently correcting her.

"Jes?" She looks surprised.

"No, you—" I point to her. "You have two girls and one boy."

She repeats what I've just said, then looks at me. "You have kids?"

"Yes, one girl. She's twenty."

"Jes." She looks back to the classroom. "You daddy, he no look good. He sick?"

Her question startles me. I think about not telling her about his cancer. Yet she has such a look of concern on her face, I open up a little.

"Yes, he was sick but he's getting better."

"What wrong?"

"He had cancer. He's in remission now." I feel the familiar closing of my throat, my chest tightening.

She touches my hand. Her fingers are as cold as mine. "Good he here. You good kid."

I smile, shuffle through the papers in front of me, try to distract myself from the tightness in my throat. She touches my hand again.

"It be okay."

I make myself look at her.

"He be okay," she says again.

"You think so?" I wonder if she's like me. Does she have feelings about things, an intuition that surprises her, too?

She pats my shoulder. "My…Daddy…he have same."

"Cancer?"

"Jes."

"Is he okay?"

Her expression grows more serious, as if she's going to tell me something very important.

"Jes…he…fine. He with God today."

"Oh" is all I can say.

I look over at Dad. We have just pulled out of the school parking lot. The dashboard light softens his sharp features and he looks almost young.

"Remember when you used to let me drive when I was a kid?" I ask. I smile, then focus on the flat dark road in front of us.

"I let you drive?"

"Yes. I drove home from the store after you bought ice cream?" I laugh. "I'll never forget that summer. Every night, you let me drive, right before you and Mom got divorced."

It always amazes me what people remember. I've asked Lena about things she and I did when we were little. Most of the time we have these separate memories, our own little movies of our pasts.

"I let you drive at ten? That wasn't such a good idea." He moves his hands to his reedlike thighs.

"I was twelve. We'd go for ice cream and, on the way home, you let me drive."

"All the way home? You weren't sitting on my lap?"

"No, by then I was too big. That's one of my best memories I have when I was a kid."

That summer, every night Dad drove eight blocks to a little grocery store for a pint of Rocky Road ice cream. One night, I was sitting on the couch crying because Lena wouldn't let me talk with her and her friend who was sleeping over. Dad walked through the living room, stopped at the front door and looked at me. He rubbed his chin, then said I could go to the store with him.

I sat in the front seat, watching the squares of house lights move by as we drove through the cool streets. On the way home, he turned to me and asked if I wanted to drive.

Did I want to drive! My twelve-year-old heart started pounding and I felt such excitement. I stared at him to see if he was serious. The dashboard light illuminated his solemn expression, in the same way it's doing now.

When I said yes, he pulled the car to the curb, put it in Park, got out and adjusted the seat. He told me to slide over. I did and he went to the other side, climbed in. My father never had much patience. He always wanted things right, but that night and the ones after, he calmly explained how to put the car in gear, how to press on the gas, brake.

For most of my life, I remember him as serious, very rarely playing games with Lena or me. On the rare occasion when he did, he corrected our behavior. But that summer, he seemed to get a kick out of me driving the eight blocks home. I never told anyone and I guess he didn't, either. A block from the house, we'd stop, I'd slide over, and he'd drive the rest of the way, then pull the car into the garage.

I felt so close to him. Each night in the garage, before we got out of the car he'd tell me I did a good job.

Now, he smiles, not big, but as if he's remembering something. "You were a good kid."

"I was?"

"Yeah, you were quiet, didn't get in much trouble. Did I ever tell you what a good kid you were?"

"No, that summer you told me I did a good job with driving."

"I was always busy...too busy. I should have taken some time." He looks out the window at the darkness. "It's so late."

"It's never too late, Dad. You told me just now."

Suddenly, I realize he's probably talking about the time, that it's after nine.

"That summer was right before your mother said she wanted a divorce, wasn't it?"

My heart was sore for years after their divorce. And for the first time, I realize how devastated he must have been—his wife leaving, everyone knowing their life together wasn't what it looked like from the outside.

"That must have been difficult for you."

"It was…I felt like…" He leans forward, takes a deep breath.

"You felt how? I don't know how I'd feel if David and I ever split."

"I felt like a failure. I thought I could fix the marriage. I was pretty hurt at that time. I never forgave your mother."

"Could you forgive her now?"

He doesn't say anything, just stares straight ahead.

"Did you have fun tonight?" I ask to fill the space, don't like thinking about my parents not caring about each other.

"Yeah. Did you make progress with Lulu?"

"I guess. I still don't know what I'm doing." I think about Lulu's and my conversation, her father's illness and the road begins to blur.

He fine. He with God today.

"You know more than you think you do, honey. I watched you tonight. You did a great job." Dad's voice is deep, smooth. "It's going to work out, you'll see. You're helping them, you care, and that's what really matters."

"But I don't know if I'm teaching the right stuff, if I'm teaching it the right way."

"Sometimes we just have to trust we're doing the right thing."

His encouragement feels good. I reach over and squeeze his hand, then turn my attention back to the road ahead.

David, Dad and I are headed to JR's Café. It's Saturday and David doesn't have to work. When I woke up, I thought it would be nice for us to go out for breakfast. Before Dad came to stay with us, David and I went out to a restaurant about once a month, and on those mornings, we seemed to talk more.

David pulls in front of JR's Café. It's a typical Texas restaurant—a plain place in a small strip mall owned by a local. Dad gets out of the back seat, opens my door and when we get to the restaurant, he holds the door for us. There's no hostess, so we take a booth by the large window that looks out onto the parking lot.

"My class is going well. Dad really helped the other night," I say to David. We are on one side of the booth, and Dad's across from us.

David nods, studies the one-page menu. "That's good. I think I'll have a Mexican omelet."

Dad stares out at the parking lot.

"You know what you want?" I ask him. He looks so tired.

"Just some oatmeal."

"You can get that at home," David says. "Have an omelet or French toast."

Dad nods.

"Did you like coming to class with me?" I ask, try to stir the conversation.

"Yeah, I did. I like the ladies."

"Want to go again?"

"Sure."

"The women are nice, aren't they?"

"Yeah, they are."

And then there is silence until the waitress comes to our table with coffee. She stands by Dad, puts her hand on his shoulder for a quick moment then perches it on her hip.

"Hey, handsome, how ya' doing?"

My father looks up, manages to smile at her, then drops his gaze to the menu. Early winter sunlight pours into the restaurant. In the bright light, I can see his skin is sallow and his face is so thin his nose looks disproportionally large.

"What would you like, handsome?" the waitress asks. Dad grimaces. With all his weight loss, he is anything but that.

"Oatmeal."

I feel his embarrassment in my chest, underneath my heart.

"Oatmeal it is." The waitress grins at him, pats his shoulder again. I know she is trying to be nice, but her remarks embarrassed him.

I swallow, pretend I'm studying the menu. Doesn't she realize my father is sick, that he used to be handsome? And I'm sure she has no idea that the back of his head still looks like Cary Grant's.

I've cornered David in our master bathroom.

"Can you believe what that waitress said to Dad?" I ask in an angry whisper. I've closed our bedroom door so my father won't hear me.

"What'd she say?"

"You didn't notice? Geez, you never pay attention. Calling him *handsome!* I can't believe some people." My hurt and anger twist together, spiral wide, and make my chest ache.

"Melinda, calm down. *Handsome* is a good word."

"I am calm." I say this, but it's not true. All my muscles are tensed. "It was so disgusting."

"She was being nice." David gives me the look he always gives me when he's frustrated with me.

"Oh, yeah, she was trying to be nice, all right, maybe she should learn some manners! She was rude. Dad looks terrible." My voice cracks and I clear my throat.

"He looks okay."

I stop, take a deep breath. "He doesn't look the same, and I want him to. I didn't realize how bad he looks till this morning. I know the woman didn't mean anything, but…" I give up trying not to cry.

"Why the hell are you crying?" David rubs his face.

"Because…because I'm worried about him. Dr. London said he has three months, then he said he might be in remission. *Might.* What a terrible word.

And that waitress." I point toward the direction of the restaurant. "She was rude!"

"Melinda," he says softly, steps toward me but I move back, put up my right hand up like a stop sign.

"I was planning on us having such a nice breakfast, a good time."

He looks at me like I'm a flat tire he has to fix. And I hate this.

"Your father seems like he's doing a lot better."

"He's always tired." Maybe all I want from David right now is a hug. But he's not affectionate, never has been. I've known this since we were married. His mother is the same way. When we first got married, it surprised me how she never hugged or kissed her son. And at our wedding she shook his hand, then mine! I guess our childhoods make indelible footprints on our souls, and we continue to walk in them for the rest of our lives.

"I thought our breakfast was fine. We talked. Your dad got out of the house. Stan probably didn't even notice what the waitress said."

"Oh, he noticed," I say, continue crying. "But I guess we did have a good time."

"Then what's wrong?"

"I don't know." Yet I do. I'm exhausted from feeling as if we are standing on the edge of a cliff looking down, and we're just about to be pushed by someone named *Cancer*.

CHAPTER SIXTEEN

My father came to my English class with me again tonight. Right now, he's working with Lupé and Sue on learning the names of household items.

Lulu and I have just come out into the hallway. We sit next to each other in the small desks. Lupé and Sue laugh. Lulu and I glance toward the classroom, then smile at each other. She has such a nice face with her dark eyes and full lips.

I glance at my notes. At the top of the list is the word *employment. Circle of Words* suggests that the instructor ask the more advanced students to talk about their work.

"What type of work do you do?" I ask.

"I keep the house." Lulu makes a circular motion with her right hand as if she's dusting.

"You're a housekeeper."

"Jes...for three peoples. I keep the houses." She nods.

"Three *people*."

"Three." With her index finger she draws three invisible houses in the air.

"You keep house for three families."

"Three *families*." She elongates the word, makes the syllables soft, warm, buttery.

"What do Lupé and Sue do?" I gesture back to the classroom.

"Do?"

"What work?"

"They keep the houses. Peoples house." She holds up her hand. "People, not peoples."

"No, when there is more than one it can be peoples."

She frowns with confusion.

"I know. English is very difficult. But you're doing well, don't worry."

"How Daddy?" She glances toward the classroom.

"He's fine."

More laughter dances to us through the closed classroom door. I get up and look into the room. My father is walking a cat picture across his desk, and the women have their hands over their lips, trying to stifle their giggles.

I come back to my desk. "They're having a good time."

"He no look good." Her expression has turned to worry.

"No, he's doing better. He's walking and eating." I nod my head, hope she will stop talking about my father. I want to focus on how much better he's doing.

"My daddy look same as Daddy when he go with God."

"No, my father's in remission." My tone is firm, yet my heart begins to beat faster and my stomach feels clenched, odd.

"I go Mexico when Daddy sick." She brings her hand to her chest, crosses herself, then she points to the classroom. "He look same, *malo*."

I know the Spanish word for "bad."

"When did he die?" Right away I'm sorry I've asked. I'm supposed to be teaching English, not talking about illness, death. And I'm determined to stay positive about my father.

She shakes her head. "He no die, he go with God." She touches her right index finger. "Two month. Then he go."

Her expression is sad, yet there is hope in her voice. I reach over and pat her shoulder. "I'm sorry."

"No sorry. He better. Before die he had…sueño."

"You mean he had cancer?"

She shakes her head, puts her hands together like she's praying, then moves them by her cheek and closes her eyes.

"He was sleeping?" I ask, confused, wish I knew Spanish.

She smiles, shakes her head again, then closes her eyes and moves her finger in a circle by her temple.

"He had a dream?"

"Jes." She smiles broadly. "He dream Mommy come. Week later he dead." She crosses herself again. "Mommy dead long time but she come for her boy."

"She did?" Surprise and doubt mix together in my body.

"Jes. Daddy saw Mommy before die. I knew he die soon."

My mother always told me stories about people dying and seeing dead relatives. I used to believe these, thought the idea so wonderful. That is until Vanessa, when I began wondering why I didn't know.

"Maybe…" I hesitate. I'm not sure Lulu would understand the word *hallucinate*. "Maybe," I put my hand to my temple, "maybe, he was—"

"*No*. He saw Mommy. Daddy afraid die. See Mommy, no afraid. You no be afraid for your daddy."

Dad is sitting in the passenger seat, his hands resting on his thighs. He's wearing his heavy Lands' End jacket and I have the heater on full-blast to fight the winter cold as we head for home. I think about what Lulu said, imagine her father with the same jet-black hair she has, lying in bed in a small house in Mexico and Lulu sitting beside him.

"Did you have a good time tonight?" I ask my father.

"Yeah, I did. I taught the ladies how to say *re...fridge...ger...ra...tor*." He enunciates each syllable then laughs.

"I heard the three of you giggling. Actually, Lupé and Sue were the ones. You looked pretty serious with that paper cat parading across your desk."

"We had a good time tonight. They're teaching me a little Spanish. *Gato negro*." His lips move into another smile as he turns his attention to the road. "I always wanted to learn Spanish. I took a class once, but I didn't have time to practice so I dropped it. Wasn't that stupid?"

"No. You were a busy man. Now you can learn."

"I feel really tired tonight."

"You can go right to bed when we get home."

"Yeah, I think I will. What did you and Lulu work on?"

"Oh, I talked to her about her work, and then a little bit about her father."

The image surfaces again, of Lulu's father lying in bed, white sheet covering him. I try to push it out of my thoughts, but it won't budge.

"What does she do?"

"She's a housekeeper. So are Lupé and Sue. Lulu says she and the others keep the *peoples* houses." I try to say the word like she did—round, smooth, beautiful.

"They must have a difficult life financially. Not knowing the language, probably no medical insurance. Some people have it hard." Dad shakes his head.

I hear the familiar empathy for other people that I've heard all my life.

"All the women are from Mexico?" Dad asks.

"I think so."

"I wonder if they still have families there?"

"I know Lulu's father lived there before he passed away." I look over and Dad smiles. The ache in my stomach grows. I turn my attention back to the road and we continue moving down the dark street.

* * *

The phone rings and I pick it up, say hello.

"Can I speak with Stanley?" It's Jan's whispery-girl voice.

I am always polite to her when she calls—I say hello, ask how she is, then get Dad on the phone. After, I walk out of the room to give him privacy.

"Hi, Jan, how are you?"

There's a long pause, but I hear her breathing.

"I'm fine, well, as good as I can be with Stanley so ill."

I take a deep breath, plunge in.

"Like I said last week, Dad's really doing a lot better. His nurse calls it a miracle. He's been going with me to an English class I'm teaching in the evenings."

Another long pause.

"Should he be out in the cold? I saw that your weather's really cold."

"He wore his heavy jacket. He's fine." I pause, tell myself not to do this, but I can't stop myself. "Could you please mail Dad his watch? I'll pay for the postage."

"His watch? I don't have his watch."

There's no way I can prove this isn't true. She

will never admit she has it. "Fine. Just a minute, I'll get Dad."

I take the phone back to his bedroom.

"Dad. It's Jan."

He gets out of bed and crosses the space between us. "Thanks, honey."

I walk to the door, stop, want to say something to him about the watch, but change my mind. He'd only put his hand over the receiver, shake his head.

"Hi, honey, how you doing?" is all I hear before I pull the door shut so he can have some privacy. As I walk down the hall I have the urge to take the phone from him, go into the kitchen, fill the sink with water and submerge the receiver.

Thirty minutes later Dad is standing across from me in the breakfast nook.

"Did you have a nice talk?" I ask, turn my attention back to the textbook.

"Yeah. She worries about me. I've told her not to, but you know Jan."

"It's nice she calls" is all I can say. I want so much for my father to be happy.

"Jan asked me to explain to you that she doesn't have my watch."

I look up, smile. "Okay. She did have your wallet,

though, when she took your car and wouldn't give it back to me. Your watch was missing right after she walked out so I assumed she has your watch."

He nods, purses his lips. "Just forget about the watch."

"Okay." Yet my anger about this embeds more deeply in my chest.

"I'm going to send Jan five hundred dollars."

"Great." I close the book and look out to the oak tree that is bathed in bright winter sunlight to hide my dissatisfaction. The pansies are still pretty and I wonder how many daffodils will bloom.

"She wants to come visit me."

I turn back to him. "That's good, Dad." But my head begins to pound. I don't want Jan in our home, walking around, leaving tea bags all over my kitchen. "You know, Dad, she and I got in an argument in Las Cruces."

"She told me about it."

Oh, God.

"It wasn't an argument on my part. She can be very hard to deal with. And I was so worried about you—"

"Yeah, I know how she is. I was married to her, honey."

I want to say, "The key word, Dad, is *was*," but I

don't. He was married to my mother, too, but they don't talk.

"I suggested she go home and she stomped off with your car, your wallet and your watch. She really screwed me over, even David thinks so."

"She's had a rough life. Her father abandoned her when she was little. She and her mother didn't have much money."

"I know, you've told me all that. I just don't think it's an excuse for the way she acted."

"We've been friends a long time, been through a lot together. After your mother left, well, Jan was the first person who I felt I could talk to. She and I just can't be married."

I cross my arms, feel like a jerk for putting my father in the middle of this, but I feel caught in the middle, too. "When is she going to visit?" I ask, make myself smile at him.

"Maybe in two weeks. I'll get her a hotel room, if you tell me where the closest one is. I'd like to show her the town, JR's Café. I'll rent a car for her. She misses Texas. Then I thought I'd go home. I'm feeling better."

A weird feeling bounces inside me, tumbles,

crashes against my bones, my muscles. I want my father to go home, but I'm still worried about him.

A miracle.

"I think that's a good idea."

"Yeah, we'll see how things work out." Dad turns, heads back to his room.

I make my way out to the front porch. The cold air and winter sunlight press against me. At the bare oak tree, I put my hand on the trunk and stare at the ground.

David and I are watching TV. My father has already gone to his room for the evening. A commercial comes on and David turns down the sound.

"How was work?" I ask.

"Like always. The Bennett project is going well. Eldon thinks I might get an award for it."

"Another? That would be wonderful."

"Yeah, it would."

"You deserve it. You work so hard, honey."

He picks up the *TV Guide* and flips the pages. My husband has earned many awards for his building designs, and each time I'm proud of him. He acts like the awards mean nothing to him, but I know they do. I guess he learned from his mother not to make a fuss.

When we were first married, my mother-in-law came to visit for her birthday. I baked a cake, bought her a sweater and cooked a special dinner. That night, after our small party was finished and I was cleaning up, she came into the kitchen, told me that their family didn't do celebrations, and I needed to take the sweater back. Later that evening, I told David, couldn't hide my shock and hurt. He shook his head, told me it would be better if I did what she asked because she wasn't going to change.

"Dad talked to Jan this afternoon," I say. "She might come visit." I want to let this bomb off slowly so David can get used to the idea. After Dad went back to his room, I realized that Jan coming to visit might help Dad feel better, and I needed to get over my hurt feelings.

"Here?" David looks at me like I've announced Fidel Castro is coming to stay at our house.

"Yeah, he said he's going to get her a hotel room."

"And he'll have to *pay* for it, too. Why the hell does he fool with her? After what she did to you?"

"David," I whisper. "I know you're right, but I don't want Dad to hear, and I don't want any problems. Her visit might make him feel better. He also said he'll go home after she leaves."

"Maybe he should *hear*. I don't know why he has anything to do with her. She's a gold digger."

I pat the air with the flat of my hand, hoping he'll lower his voice.

"She's nutty, I know. She did try to help him." I whisper, try to soft-pedal my feelings about Jan.

"You should tell him what she did to you, with his car, his frigging watch."

"David, don't yell. I did tell him."

"But I know you. You probably said, 'Oh, it was okay.'"

"I didn't want to make him feel bad. He's in such a good mood right now. You have no idea what it was like in Las Cruces because you wouldn't come and help me."

He gives me that look I know so well, that *we aren't going to go there* look.

"Jan jacked you around. I don't like it when people take advantage of you. And the Skillys didn't do much to help you, either." He puts the *TV Guide* back on the end table. "What's going to stop her from stealing something in our house?"

"I think she took Dad's things because...I don't really think she's a thief, just unstable. If she comes to visit, I don't want Dad to feel uncomfortable. We can put up with her for a little while."

"All I'm saying is, what about you?"

I stand. "I know, but we'll just have to deal with this. Maybe she'll change her mind about coming." I walk into the dark kitchen, stare out the window at the oak tree. The wind blows and the naked branches bend with the invisible force.

CHAPTER SEVENTEEN

The three of us are sitting in the family room watching "Wheel of Fortune." Dad just solved the puzzle. The clue was *a thing* and Dad said wedding ring before David or I could.

"That was great, Dad. I think I'll do the dishes. You both are too good at this." I get up from the couch, head toward the kitchen.

"Let me do them, honey," Dad says.

I stop beside his chair. He looks so tired. "You don't have to. There aren't many. Watch TV, beat David some more."

"No. You cooked. *I'll* do the dishes." He brings his hand to his chest in an exaggerated gesture I've seen so many times.

"Okay, if you aren't too tired."

Dad's been doing the dishes for the past few days. He offered and I think it makes him feel better, useful. Yesterday he helped me clean out the kitchen pantry and organize all the food boxes and cans alphabetically. But then that wore him out and he slept all afternoon.

"I'll do the dishes." He gets up from his chair, takes two steps toward the kitchen, but stops, grabs his head with both hands and his anguished expression scares me.

"What is it?" I walk over, touch his shoulder.

"That was a weird feeling."

"What do you mean, weird? Are you in pain?" My heart thumps hard and I look toward David. He's muted the TV and he's staring at us.

"Just weird. Like a cracking in my head."

"Do you want a Motrin or a pain pill? Is it like a headache?"

"No. It was just a weird feeling." He walks into the kitchen. My stomach tightens into a hard knot and I glance at David again.

He mouths "go check."

I find Dad next to the sink. He turns on the water, begins rinsing our dishes, putting them in the dishwasher.

"Are you sure you're okay?"

"Yeah, honey, I'm fine." But the lines around his mouth and the feeling in my chest tells me he isn't.

* * *

I am sitting in Dr. London's waiting room trying to read a *People* magazine, but I can't concentrate. A few moments ago the receptionist took Dad back to one of the exam rooms. I called her early this morning, insisted on an appointment right away so Dad could explain to the doctor how his head felt last night.

On the end table next to me I notice a tiny sign that states Dr. London is president of the Medical Doctors' Association for Hypnosis. I pick it up, turn it over. It says that hypnosis can be used for pain reduction and relaxation. I put the sign back on the table. My father used to be interested in hypnosis, years ago, when I was a kid. He tried to hypnotize my sister when she was twelve, but she wouldn't stop giggling long enough, so he gave up.

He was always trying different things. Another year, he set the stereo on a timer so a record would play when he and Mom were sleeping. When I asked him what he was doing, Dad explained it was a form of hypnosis, listening to subliminal calming messages. He did this every evening, until my mother told him she couldn't sleep with all the clicks and buzzings in the middle of the night.

"Melinda."

I find the voice. The receptionist is standing in the doorway to the exam rooms. She motions me to her. The two people in the waiting room glance up from their magazines.

I stand, smile at them.

"Yes?" I whisper when I get to her.

"Dr. London would like to see you."

"Okay."

My father is sitting on the examination table with his shirt off. His shoulders look so bony. Dr. London is standing next to him. I walk into the room and shut the door behind me.

"Hi," I say.

"Have you noticed your father's been lisping?"

"No." I look at Dad. He's clutching his thighs, staring at the floor.

"Mr. Howard, say light."

My father looks up and I see fear in his eyes.

"Light," my father says.

There is a little lisp, as if he's had one too many beers.

"Did you hear the lisp?" Dr. London asks.

I nod. "Are you okay, Dad?" I step close to him, cover his hand with mine. He's trembling.

"Can you take your father to an oncologist today? I want him examined immediately."

"Of course. That's no problem." I feel the familiar numbness working its way through my body, spreading across my chest, into my arms, my legs. I thought my father was doing okay, getting better.

"I'll have Janice call. Maybe Dr. Darby can see you this afternoon." He turns again to my father, touches his shoulder. "We'll let you put your shirt on, Mr. Howard."

Dr. London motions me to go ahead of him, out into the hallway. He closes the door and we walk toward the waiting room. I stop before we get to the exit.

"What do you think is wrong?" A tiny bit of hope wraps itself around my chest. Maybe what's wrong can be fixed and Dad will be okay.

"I'm not sure, but it's probably not good. I'm sorry."

We are driving down Lancaster Boulevard, a busy Fort Worth street, trying to find Dr. Darby's office. Dad hasn't spoken a word since we left Dr. London's office.

"I don't know where the hell this place is. You know, you'd think doctors, with all the money they make, would have bigger signs so a person could find their offices."

I immediately feel awful for raising my voice, being cranky. Dad stares straight ahead, his hands on his thighs. Finally, I see the sign for the doctor on the left side of the street.

"There it is. Well, now that we're here that wasn't so bad."

I pull into the small parking lot, lean back, close my eyes and take a deep breath to calm myself. A moment later I look at my father. He is sitting very still.

"Are you ready to go in?" I ask, and immediately realize what a stupid question this is. Who in their right mind is ever ready to go to an oncologist?

He doesn't move.

"Dad?" I say softly. My face and hands begin to tingle.

"Yeah?"

"If you don't want to go in, we don't have to. Really. You don't have to do anything you don't want to. We can go home, come back later. We'll watch TV, have some dinner. David said he might be home early tonight so the three of us can watch 'Wheel of Fortune.' We always have fun doing that."

Dad shakes his head. "No, we'd better go hear what the fine doctor has to say."

The tiny lisp is there. How did it come on him so fast? And why didn't I notice it? I close my eyes, grip the steering wheel, try to calm myself.

Dear God, please make my father okay, please, oh, please.

I open my eyes and look at him. I love him so much. I climb out of the car, go around to the other side and open his door. Dad gets out and I put my arm around him, hug him. "You know I love you, don't you?"

"Yeah, I know that. I love you, too, honey."

I wonder if I've ever told him this before. I'm sure I have, but right now I can't remember.

We break apart. I take his arm and golden afternoon sun washes over us.

"It's going to be all right," I say.

"Oh, I don't think so." His tone is not sad but matter-of-fact.

I stare at the concrete and the sun anoints the back of my head, my neck.

Dear God, please, let my father be okay.

Dad is waiting to be called back to an exam room. We've been in Dr. Darby's office for over two and a half hours. Forty minutes after we got here, she examined him then ordered X-rays of my father's head. Technicians did the X-rays in another part of the building and now we are back in her waiting room.

"Mr. Howard," the receptionist says. She's standing by the door with a large envelope in her hand. Dad gets up, turns to me.

"Will you come with me?"

"Sure," I say, but I want to drive home, climb into bed, pull the blankets over my head and forget this ever happened.

We follow the nurse back to the exam room.

"Just have a seat. Dr. Darby will be with you in a moment."

She walks into the hallway, leaves the door open. I hear two women laughing and I wonder what they are so happy about. Dad sits on the exam table. I take a chair by the small sink. Neither of us says a word.

A few minutes later Dr. Darby walks in. She is about thirty-seven with dark hair and pretty blue eyes.

"Hello again, Mr. Howard."

"Hello," Dad says.

I stand, extend my hand. "I'm Melinda, his daughter."

She shakes my hand, looks very serious and my heart begins to race.

"Okay." She turns on the three white plastic boxes hooked to the wall.

My father stares at them. She reaches over, turns off the fluorescent light. And we are illuminated in eerie moonlight.

I close my eyes, grip the sides of the chair.

God, *please, let my father be okay.*

When I open my eyes she is clipping the last of three X-rays onto the lighted boxes.

"You see here." She points to my father's X-rayed skull in the first black-and-white image.

A large lump the size of a peach pit has embedded itself in his skull. I blink. The small irregular circle looks as if it's waiting for spring and the sun so it can sprout.

My father's expression is anguished. I turn away, stare at my hands for a moment to compose myself. But it doesn't help. I begin sniffing back tears.

"Radiation might shrink them." She points to another slightly smaller peach pit, two inches away from the larger one.

My father turns his attention to his clenched hands.

"Are you experiencing any pain?"

Dad shakes his head. "Just that cracking. But no pain."

God, he's been through so much.

"If you don't have any pain, I would suggest you not do radiation. There can be complications from it."

Dad nods.

"I'll send Dr. London a letter and he can discuss your condition with you." She turns a little and Dad looks up again. It's as if she's dusting off her hands, telling us silently there's nothing else anyone can do.

I *should* ask her what those lumps are going to do, but I don't have to. I know. The cancer never stopped. It was only hiding, playing games with us. If I ask questions we'll only get *maybes*, *guesses* of how many months, weeks, and stupid instructions on staying positive.

"Okay," I say. "Thank you."

She walks out into the hallway, doesn't glance back, then disappears. Dad stands and so do I. He takes my arm and we walk out of the room.

In the waiting area five people are sitting close together, forming a circle. Two of the women are holding hands and their fear is palpable. I know these feelings well. The fear has wound its way around my heart, across my shoulders, even under my fingernails, leaving its imprint on my soul. I can feel it now.

I straighten, take a deep breath. These people are waiting for news, and most times good news does not come out of this kind of office. I soften my gaze, silently tell them I'm sorry. Then I squeeze my father's arm and we head for home.

First Week in March

"I'm going to quit my teaching job," I say to David. He's just come into the kitchen from the garage. It's nine-thirty. I ate dinner alone an hour ago. Dad had a piece of toast at six, washed it down with a third of a glass of milk and then went back to bed. Now I'm washing our few dishes.

"What?" he asks.

I repeat what I said, watch our wavy reflections in the kitchen window. David looks tired. He's unbuttoned the first two buttons of his shirt, his tie hangs loose and he's holding his suit jacket over his shoulder.

"Why would you do that? Don't you like the job anymore?"

"I love it."

It has been two weeks since we were in Dr. Darby's office. Now Dad stays in bed most of the time and his lisp is getting worse.

"Then why would you quit?"

"Dad needs me," I whisper.

"Yeah, I know he does."

"And I'm afraid to leave him alone. Tonight I had to help him into his pajamas because he's so tired." I cross my arms, press my lips together. "He's so weak."

David crosses the kitchen, stands next to me. I see more fatigue in his eyes.

"How can I leave him alone? I just can't do it. I've come to feel so responsible for him." Many times a day I go to his room, ask him if he wants anything to eat or drink. Sometimes he does, most of the times he doesn't.

About a week ago he asked me to take care of his bills and help him with what little paperwork he has. He said it makes him too tired to write checks. More and more, my life is melting into his.

"I'm afraid he's going to fall. It would be awful if that happened when I was gone."

"I know, but I don't think you should stop teaching. You enjoy the class. You always talk about your students."

I dry my hands, face him.

"I don't want to quit, but what can I do? If I don't go and check on him, he calls for me. I think he's afraid to be alone."

"I'm here most of the time when you have to go to school." David glances at the oven clock.

"But sometimes you aren't. I can't depend on you being home."

"What if I promise to come home early the nights you have to teach?"

"You would do *that?*" I try to hide the surprise in my voice. David has always been so conscientious about his work, so devoted, too much so, sometimes.

"Yeah, I would. The teaching's been good for you. It's nice you enjoy it. And I want your dad to be safe." David gestures back toward Dad's room.

"What nights do I teach?" I ask, then laugh because I know he won't remember.

"Tuesdays and Thursdays. If I promise I'll be home before you have to leave, will you keep teaching?"

David is always good on his promises, but I hate to infringe on his work, his time. "Oh, you don't have to do that."

"Melinda, I'm beginning to think there are more important things than work."

"What if something at the office comes up and they need you?"

"I'll deal with it the next day. There should be some benefit to being a partner, don't you think?"

"Yeah, I do."

CHAPTER EIGHTEEN

"Daddy no here?" Lulu asks, glances at the classroom door.

It's six forty-five. We are already sitting in our circle. The women arrived before I did and arranged the desks, put Dad's desk with ours.

David got home at six, and he and I ate a quick dinner before I left. Dad was already in bed. The only time he gets up now is to go to the bathroom or to go to Dr. London' office. He's eating very little and when he does, I take a tray to his room.

Before I left for school, I went back and told him where I was going, explained David was home. He smiled, told me to drive carefully and to tell the ladies *hola* for him. I asked him if he wanted to come with me, but he just shook his head.

I glance at the empty desk then at my students. They are looking at me with such concern. I have not told them what we know about Dad's health.

"Dad asked me to tell you *hola*. He's not feeling well tonight."

"Daddy *malo?*" Lulu asks.

"Yes." I draw in a breath. "Very *malo*."

Lulu says something in Spanish to Lupé and Sue. They shake their heads, talk a little in Spanish. I have the urge to say, *"English, English,"* but that would be silly.

"Where you live?" Lulu leans forward.

I explain where. Our town is so small everyone knows our subdivision.

"We come see Daddy." Lulu nods and the other two women do, too.

"You would visit him?"

"Jes. We come. Daddy help *us*." She makes a circling motion with her hand to include Lupé and Sue.

I'm not sure my father wants company, but he seems so lonely. My sister only calls on the weekends when the rates are low. Jan still calls, but she and Dad don't talk as long as they used to. And there is no one else to visit except Elizabeth and these three women.

"Yes, please come and see him. I know my father would like that. Anytime, you don't have to call."

* * *

Dad and I arrived at Dr. London's office an hour ago and the receptionist told us it would only be a few minutes. Then, a half hour later, she said the doctor had an emergency and it would be a little longer. By then, Dad was slumped in the chair. Finally the nurse called him back to the exam room.

This morning, I had to punch an extra hole in his belt with a knife because he's gotten so skinny. And he asked me to hold his shirt as he slipped his arms through the sleeves. I didn't want to bring him here today because he seemed exhausted, but he insisted that he wanted to see Dr. London.

Weeks ago, I showed Dad the tiny sign for the hypnosis treatment and asked him if he wanted to try it. He said he did. Dr. London explained hypnosis would be a great tool for Dad to relax or to use for pain.

Dad and Dr. London have now done two hypnosis sessions and both sessions were taped. I thought Dad could listen to the tapes at home. So today, again, I brought a small tape recorder and a blank tape. I set it up, then gave it to Dad before he went into the doctor's office.

The door to the inner rooms opens and the receptionist smiles at me.

"Dr. London would like to see you."

I find the doctor standing in the middle of his office. Dad is sitting in the chair in front of his desk. My tape recorder rests on the mahogany desk.

"Thanks for taping," I say, walk to the desk, pick up the tape recorder and clutch it to my chest. Dr. London's serious expression makes my heartbeat quicken.

"Is something wrong? Did everything go okay?"

He motions to the other chair next to my father, but I don't want to sit.

"Your father says he's tired."

"Yes, he's told me."

"We've completed the hypnosis sessions and we've talked. We both feel he doesn't need to come back to my office for any more appointments."

"Not come back? He really likes you."

Dr. London nods, smiles. "I like your father, too, but I received Dr. Darby's letter." He gestures to the file on his desk. "Your father's cancer is progressing and it's going to make him very tired. The drive down here might be too much for him."

Progressing—the word sounds so positive.

"Maybe we could come earlier in the morning. He has more energy then."

The words spill over the huge lump in my throat, out into the room, circle us. I know Dad's tired, but I don't want him to lose this, too. He's told me he likes talking to his doctor.

Dr. London shakes his head. "Not at this stage."

Dad has been staring at his lap the entire time. I grip the tape recorder hard. I am not ready to give up, not like this.

"If he feels better next week, I'll drive him down here. Thanks for making the tapes."

Dad struggles out of the chair, takes my arm. We walk all the way out of the office into the bright winter sunlight before I can take a deep breath.

Someone just knocked on the front door. I'm sitting in the family room and the noise startled me. Most people who come to our house ring the bell. I get up, walk to the door and look through the side light window. Lulu and Lupé are standing on the porch in afternoon sunlight. They are both holding grocery bags. I open the door.

"Hi!" I motion them in. "I'm so glad to see you."

"Hello," they say at the same time, and all three of us laugh.

"How are you?" I ask.

"Fine," Lulu says, and Lupé nods.

They follow me to the kitchen. I take Lupé's bag, place it on the kitchen counter and Lulu places hers next to it. "What did you bring?"

"Food. We came see Daddy," Lulu says.

"That's so nice of you. I know he'll enjoy seeing both of you."

"And see you," Lupé adds. "We bring enchiladas for husband." She points to the paper bags.

"Thank you. It's so good to have company."

My days are so much the same now. I get up, help my father to the bathroom, then he goes back in bed. I bring him a small glass of milk and a piece of toast. After David goes to work, I check on Dad, watch TV, plan my lessons for Tuesdays and Thursdays, or wait for Elizabeth if she is scheduled to visit. Usually, I have no energy or care about cleaning the house, but sometimes I make myself do it anyway.

David comes home at different times, and he and I watch more TV. Then I help my father brush his teeth, get back into bed, and we start all over the next day.

"You like enchiladas?" Lulu gestures to the brown grocery bag.

"Oh, yes. I love them."

"Daddy eat?"

I shake my head. "He hasn't been eating very much."

"Ah," Lupé says, "we brings soup." She pulls out a large yellow Tupperware container.

"This is so nice of you," I say, bathe in their goodness.

"You have enchiladas," Lulu says. "Daddy soup."

"Yes, my husband and I will have them for dinner before school."

They smile, nod.

"Would you like to see my father now?"

"Jes," Lulu says.

"He might be asleep. Why don't you sit in the living room and I'll tell him you're here." I gesture to the living room, and Lulu and Lupé sit on the couch, next to each other.

Dad's room is bright with sunlight. He is lying on his back with his eyes closed, and his hands are folded on his chest, but I don't think he's asleep.

"Dad?"

He looks at me.

"Lupé and Lulu are here to see you."

He blinks, pushes himself up on his elbow and

smiles. He hasn't smiled in days and this makes me
feel better.

"Somebody's here? Again?" He glances around
the room.

"Yes, the women from my English class came to
see you. They brought food. They want to say hello.
Isn't that wonderful?"

"Yeah, nice." He sits up a little more, smoothes
his pajama top.

"I'll go get them." I pull the chair close to the bed.

"I miss seeing the ladies."

"I know you do. They miss you, too. That's why
they came to visit."

I practically run down the hall, find Lulu and
Lupé where I left them in the living room. They are
talking in Spanish whispers.

"Dad's awake." I'm out of breath. "He's so happy
you're here. He hasn't had any company."

The women stand and I grab a chair from the
dining room.

"I carry." Lulu tries to take the chair from me.

"No, no. I'll carry it. It's so nice of you to come."
As we head down the hall, I notice Dad's doorway
is full of bright light. They follow me in and I put
the chair beside the other one.

"Please." I motion for them to sit.

Dad smiles, looks at them as if they are Christmas packages waiting to be opened.

"Hello, Daddy." Lulu moves to the bed and takes my father's left hand.

"How are you ladies doing?" His voice is strong, but the lisp rounds every word, makes him sound drunk.

I stand by the door to give them more room.

Lupé steps closer. "*Hola*, Daddy." She looks back to me as if she's made a mistake speaking Spanish.

I smile, nod, give her my approval.

"Are you ladies practicing your English?"

I hope they don't hear the lisp. Dad would be so embarrassed at this. He always spoke so well.

"Jes," Lulu answers. "We practice for Daddy. You help us. You good man."

Dad smiles again. "You sound like you've been practicing. I'm proud of you."

I go out into the hall, lean against the wall, listen to them laugh and my throat knots, twists with tears, but I manage to sniff them back.

David and I are eating dinner early. He came home from work sooner than I expected and we are having the enchiladas.

After the women talked to my father for about fifteen minutes, they came out and told me he was tired and needed to rest. While they were visiting with Dad, I unloaded the grocery bags. There were enchiladas, rice, beans, plus they'd brought a chocolate cake that Sue had made and a bag of chocolate kisses.

Lulu explained in her broken English how to heat the enchiladas. She touched my waist with her left hand, said, "Eat, eat, too small," then frowned and shook her head.

I offered them lunch but they refused, said they needed to go back to work. Lupé, right before she left, pantomimed that I should go lay down and sleep. Then both women hugged me goodbye. After they'd gone, I went back and checked on Dad. He'd already fallen asleep.

"These are good," David says around a mouthful of enchilada.

"It was so nice they came to see Dad. They even brought a homemade chocolate cake."

"Great. I stopped and got something for Stan, too."

"What?" I turn my head a little, wonder what in the world he could bring home for my father.

"I picked him up a wheelchair." He leans back and smiles.

"A wheelchair? From where?"

"The hospital supply store downtown. All he ever does is stay in that bedroom. The guy's got to be bored, lonely. I was thinking he could push himself around the house in it, maybe go out on the back porch. That way he'd have some privacy, yet get some fresh air."

I guess David doesn't realize how weak my father is. I reach over and pat his hand.

"Thanks, that was really nice of you. But Dad's pretty weak. I don't think he'll be able to do any of that."

"It would do him some good to get out of that bedroom."

I shake my head.

"What?" David asks.

"I'm losing perspective. It's as if I don't see the world in the same way anymore, you know. Lupé and Lulu came over this afternoon, and I was so happy...you would have thought it was the president visiting. I forget how isolated we are."

"I know this is hard for you."

"I'm okay." I study my husband, see the worry in

his face, how concerned he is. Once this would have bothered me, given me a feeling of claustrophobia, but now I realize how lucky I am to have a husband who worries about me, who really cares.

It's been five days since Dr. London told us Dad didn't need to come back to his office. Right now, I am waiting for Elizabeth. She phoned last night and said we would be her first visit this morning. Earlier, I helped Dad to the bathroom, waited by the closed door and then guided him back to bed. I asked if he wanted breakfast. He shook his head, said he only wanted to sleep.

From the kitchen window I see Elizabeth's blue car turn into our driveway. It's a beautiful morning, clear—the kind of day that reminds me that spring is just around the corner.

I go to the door, open it right before Elizabeth steps onto the front porch. The air is colder than I expect and the porch is lit with dazzling sunlight.

Elizabeth sees me and smiles. She's wearing a pink shirt and white pants, looks so fresh, like spring.

"How's your dad?" she asks as she walks into the house.

"He's sleeping a lot."

I gesture to his bedroom as we walk into the kitchen.

"That's the cancer. It makes patients very tired. I'm going to up my visits to three times a week since he's not seeing Dr. London on a regular basis."

"Okay." This is just another change I don't want for my father, another thing that breaks my heart, but what else can we do? "Would you like coffee?"

"Yeah, I would. I've only got five patients to see today so I have time."

We go into the kitchen and I pour the coffee I made fifteen minutes ago, take the mugs to the breakfast table. I give her the mug Jennifer gave me that Easter we were so happy eating jellybeans.

"How are you doing?" she asks, takes a sip of coffee. "You look really tired."

"I'm fine."

"Are you getting any sleep?"

"Yeah, once I help Dad get ready for bed, I sleep like a rock."

"He'll get more tired, more detached. That's the natural progression of cancer."

She seems so centered, and a tiny bit of awe

mixed with anger wells in my chest. I wouldn't be able to handle her work, act like all this is an everyday occurrence.

"How do you do this job?" I ask. "I mean, how do you watch people die? I couldn't do it, not like you, be so calm, so accepting."

She blinks, leans back. "It's difficult, but I like helping people. In a way it's like birthing a baby except I'm at the other end of the circle." She draws a small, invisible circle on the table with her right index finger.

"Elizabeth, circles don't have endings."

"They don't, but I believe life doesn't, either. When we die, our spirits live on."

"When you're dead, you're dead," I whisper. "Pretty crummy ending if you ask me. When we had to go to Dr. Darby's office, I prayed Dad would be okay. I mean, I really asked that he'd get through this. That obviously didn't work." I point back to my father's room.

"I know this is hard for you. Sometimes we don't know how or when our prayers are answered."

"Well, this time it didn't work. I would find your job so depressing."

"At times it is. It's a challenge to stay positive. I just hope I help people."

"Helping them die? How do you do stay positive through that, for God's sake?"

Elizabeth turns her head a little. "Because I don't think we die. I believe our spirits leave our tired bodies behind. I want to help people make the transition by being kind, listening to them, helping their families."

"I couldn't do it. How did you ever decide to take this on?"

Elizabeth bites her lip for a moment. "I've never told any of our friends here this, but when Brad and I were first married, we lost a child. Amanda was only six months."

I stare at her, stunned by this revelation, realize we never know anyone fully. "I'm so sorry."

"The day she passed away, I swore I would help other people. That's why I went to nursing school, then decided to work for hospice."

"I'm so sorry," I whisper, feel like a shit for being frustrated with her, with everything, but there is a part of me, the hope I held for so long, that I don't want to fade.

"That was fifteen years ago. I'm okay now, but if I thought my daughter's spirit didn't exist, I don't think I could go on, you know?"

I take a sip of coffee, let her words sink in. "It's just hard for me to believe there's anything after this life. I used to, a long time ago, but…"

"I know there's something on the other side. I've seen and heard too many things not to believe that. You know, I dream about my daughter on her birthday every year. How can you explain that?"

I think about my intuition, that feeling of knowing something for sure, and my dreams that predict, that I can't deny. How do I explain all that?

"Guess there are some things we can't explain. But maybe on your daughter's birthday, you think about her and that's why you have a dream."

Elizabeth takes another sip of coffee, touches my hand.

"I think about Amanda every day. Some people feel sorry for me because of the job I have, but I'm the lucky one. I get to see life close up, meet people who are on the edge of the biggest event in their lives. If you saw what I have, you might believe."

"What have you seen?" I want to untangle and answer all the questions inside of me.

"Just last week I was with a woman whose two granddaughters were with her when she passed. After, one of the girls told me she saw an angel above her grandmother's bed. The other girl told her mother the same thing, but in another room. Neither had talked to each other about it."

"Oh, right! They were just making it up or they were stressed, imagining."

"No they weren't. They're twelve and thirteen, very honest, calm girls. Later, we were in the living room and started talking, comparing. One girl described the same face without hearing what her sister had said. Their mother showed them a picture of the grandmother's sister who the girls had never seen. It was her."

"I don't know, Elizabeth...why..." But I have chill bumps on my arms. "Since college, I've always thought that this is it, the end of the line." I rub my eyes, feel exhausted. "I just want my father to be better."

Elizabeth reaches over and touches my hand.

"I can get you some help to come in. Are you sure you're doing okay? You know if you need anything, hospice can help."

I sit straighter, blink. "No, I'm okay, really." But I'm not. I feel like I'm hanging by a thread.

"But if you do, will you let me know?"

"Of course. Don't worry about me."

She stands. "I'd better go check on your dad."

I get up, watch Elizabeth walk down the hall to my father's room. His door is open and the area looks unnaturally bright, flooded with light.

This morning when I went to check on him, he asked me to close the shades so he could sleep. I walk down the hall, go into Dad's room. Elizabeth is standing by his bed and Dad is looking up at her. Both shades are up and sunlight is pouring through the windows.

I take a deep breath, relax a little.

Elizabeth turns toward me, smiles her sweet smile and, for a moment, she looks just like an angel.

CHAPTER NINETEEN

I'm lying in bed. The clock reads five-fifteen. David is snoring lightly, the sound comforts me. Yesterday Elizabeth had a hospital bed delivered for Dad. She explained he would be safer and more comfortable in it.

A hospital bed.

I was stunned and told her I felt it was just another part of my father's life being stripped away. After the hospital bed was delivered, Elizabeth lifted the railings, said I should keep them up, so there wouldn't be a chance that Dad could fall out of bed. Last night after helping him get into his pajamas, I pulled up the rails, and for a moment I felt like I was standing by Jenny's crib. It was an odd feeling that took me a moment to shake. I stood by the edge for a long time, asked Dad if he wanted me to have the hospital bed taken back to the supply store. He closed his eyes, said he was fine with the bed, but I don't think he is.

Now, in the bathroom I look in the mirror. Black

mascara is smeared under my eyes. I was too tired last night to take it off, so now I look like a raccoon. I hear a rattling noise then a muffled thunk. I rush out of the bedroom, stop, grab my robe. David stirs, looks at me with sleepy eyes.

"What's wrong?" he mumbles, closes his eyes again.

"I'm not sure. I heard a weird noise."

"Come back to bed, it's too early to get up."

"I can't." I rush down the hall to my father's room. Dad is lying on the floor, on his side, and my heart crashes into my ribs.

"Oh, my God, are you okay?" I kneel next to him.

"I'm okay." The lisp thickens his words, makes him sound childlike. I put my arm around him.

"What happened?"

He manages to sit up. His arms and legs look like spring tree branches—thin, fragile, breakable.

"I wanted to get out of bed."

I look at the bed. "But, Dad, the bedrails are still up. Did you forget that you're in a hospital bed?" I gesture to it.

"No, I wanted to go to the bathroom."

"And you climbed over the railing?"

"Yeah. Could you leave them down? They're really hard to climb over."

"They're not meant to climb over."

"I didn't want to bother you."

"But…"

His serious expression seems to reach in and grab the tired insanity that has been swirling inside me for weeks—all the feelings I've pushed down for weeks. We look at each other. Surprisingly, I begin to laugh and so does he.

"You could have really hurt yourself."

"How am I going to hurt myself any more than what the cancer is doing?"

"You wouldn't want to break a leg or an arm, would you?"

"I want to get out of bed when I need to."

"Call me and I'll come and help you." I help him off the floor. He holds on to me as we walk to the bathroom. When we come back to his bed, I lower the rails and we sit on the bed's edge.

"These are really tough to climb over." He touches the metal railing with his fingertips.

The only thing I know for sure is I want my father to be happy.

"I'll leave them down. Elizabeth won't like it, but I'll leave them down."

"I had a tough time getting over them."

Suddenly, I start laughing again, this time hysterically. Laughter bubbles out of me. I put my hand over my mouth in an effort to staunch it, but it doesn't help.

Dad laughs and I put my arm around him and hug him. He hugs back, and we laugh more. A drop of saliva falls onto my white robe, turns into a tiny gray circle.

A moment later our laughter is gone and I feel tingly, lighter.

Dad climbs back into bed.

"I'll leave the rails down. I'm sorry you had trouble with them."

"Thanks, honey." He rests his hands on his chest, closes his eyes.

"You sure you're okay? No aches or pains?"

He stares at me, but it's as if he's looking through me not at me.

"I'm sorry," he says.

"About falling out of bed? Don't be silly. I'm just glad you're not hurt, that everything is okay."

He grabs my forearm. "No, I mean, I'm sorry for all this."

"Oh, Dad, we're doing okay."

"No, for everything. I should have spent more

time with you when I was healthy. Now you've got to deal with this, and all alone."

I touch the edge of the sheet, feel the soft material under my fingers. This is all I've wanted for so long—my father saying he regrets not being closer, but right now it doesn't seem to matter.

"Well, we're together now," I say. "That's all that counts." And for the first time since he let me drive his car when I was twelve, I feel really close to him.

It's Saturday and I'm standing in the kitchen wondering what I should fix for dinner. The phone rings. It's probably my sister Lena. She's been calling on Saturdays, in the afternoon because the rates are lower. Most times, she talks to Dad for about ten minutes and then unloads on me with her problems.

"Hello?"

"Hi. How's Dad?" Lena asks.

"Not good. He's not eating much."

I walk into the breakfast nook, look out at the sunshine, clear sky, the ring around the tree where the daffodils are hiding.

"Is he getting out, walking?"

"No, Lena, he isn't. He can barely get out of bed. In fact, he fell out of bed yesterday."

She has no idea what Dad is like now, how fragile, how small his world has become. I guess no one does except the people who come to see him.

"Oh, my God, is he okay?"

"Yes, his nurse came and examined him. Thankfully, he didn't hurt himself."

"I…wish…"

I hear her sniff then begin to cry. My anger rises. I want to yell at her, demand she come to see him, but I know my father would have more compassion than this.

"What do you wish, Lena?"

"I just wish he were better."

"So do I. You should come and see him, Lena. I know he'd like you here. You're his daughter, too."

I feel familiar heat building in my chest, my deep need to protect my father.

"You know I can't fly," Lena says.

"Then drive, but come." I touch the window, leave a smudge mark, but I don't care. "You could take the train. Dad would really like to see you. The women from my English class came to see him and he got such a kick out of it."

"I'm…I'm just too sick. My nerves are really bad right now because I'm so worried about Dad."

And I feel sorry for her, like Dad would tell me I should—like he would. "I know, Lena, but you need to see him, for your own sake."

She cries harder and I know she won't come.

"I'll try to visit," she says between her sobs. "I will, I promise. Can I speak to Dad?"

"I hope you do come. I'll get Dad for you. He loves it when you call. Just a minute."

I walk down the hall to his room. He is lying in bed on his side, looking out the window.

"Dad, it's Lena."

He turns, smiles and there's a little excitement in his gaze. "Thanks, honey."

I give him the phone and they begin talking, Dad telling her he's doing okay. I walk back down the hallway, think about my sister. Three years after my parents adopted Lena, my mother found out she was pregnant with me, and the four of us became a pieced-together family, like all families are, just in different ways. On my birthday, Mom always told the story of how, after I was born, and they were bringing me home from the hospital, Lena sat in the back seat and screamed that they should take me back, that she didn't want a baby sister.

Years ago, our family fragmented—my mother

and father's divorce, Lena and all her problems, me staying in the background, not wanting to deal with anything that didn't seem perfect.

I stand in the breakfast nook, stare at the phone— our lifeline. Yesterday, Jan called. I asked when she was going to visit. She said she couldn't, that my father told her not to come. I wonder if that's true. If Dad was at my sister's or with Jan, I would visit, try to help.

Mr. Skilly quit calling two weeks ago when he found out how much sicker Dad had become. Thinking about my father and his illness from a distance must be difficult, and facing one's mortality through the illness of a friend must be very chilling. But these are still fragile excuses.

Before all this began, I avoided similar situations, too. *Before all this began*—that seems like a million years ago. Someone at school or the library would tell me about their mother's illness and I would say how sorry I was, but I never really connected.

I go to the front door, walk outside, stand in the middle of the yard and stare at the vast blue sky. The air is still cold, yet the winter sun warms my face.

The world is so beautiful.

Our neighbor, five doors down, drives by in his

white Ford Explorer, leans over the passenger seat and waves to me. I raise my hand, move it back and forth. He has no idea what is going on inside our house—my sister crying, my father's lisp, the ache inside my heart. The hard parts of our lives are always buried deep, coming out only when we open up.

Again I turn my face to the sun, absorb its warmth, and press my palms together. When someone tells me about a family member or friend who is sick, I will take their hands, hold them tight and look into their eyes. I will say how sorry I am. Then I'll offer to come and sit with them, just be there so they aren't alone, and they will know someone cares. Today I really mean it.

David is standing at his bathroom sink, washing his hands.

"Why won't anyone come and see him?" I lean against the counter.

"Not everyone is as nice as you, Melinda." He shakes his head, wipes his hands on the beige hand towel.

"I wish I wasn't so nice. And I wish my sister or the Skillys would come and visit him. He gets so excited when people call, when my students are here."

He touches my shoulder for a moment. "You're a good person, that's the way you are. That's why I love you."

I look at him, love him more than usual. "I appreciate how you've helped, been here for Dad and me."

"I know you do."

I walk through our bedroom, into the hallway, look toward Dad's room. It's early, but the doorway seems to be filled with bright sunlight. In his room, I find the window shades down, Dad lying on his back, staring at the ceiling, his arms down at his sides.

"Dad?"

He looks over, sees me and smiles.

"Hi, honey." He moves over a little so I can sit on the edge of his bed and I take his hand.

"Are you okay?"

"Yeah, fine." His lisp curves his words, as it has done for weeks.

He never complains, never talks about his illness. And every day I wonder what he's thinking. At night, when it's dark and the house is silent, what goes through his mind?

"You know, I had a weird dream." He sits up a little.

"You did?"

"Yeah, I was in the back seat of this big car, and it was making wild turns though a strange city, going too fast around these tall buildings." He shifts a little. "I leaned over the front seat to tell the driver to slow down or let me drive. The driver was my brother Raymond. He smiled, told me I should sit back, that everything was going to be okay, and he would drive me to where I was going."

"What did you do?"

"I felt better. Then I woke up. You know, Raymond died when he was twenty-one."

I nod, remember stories about the uncle I never met. "How old were you?" I take his hand again, rub his fingers.

"Seventeen. He was killed in a car wreck. He was my best friend."

My mother had told me stories about Raymond, how my father and he left home when they were teens because they didn't get along with their stepmother. They lived over a grocery store for three years until Raymond was killed.

A *dream*.

Sometimes they come true.

CHAPTER TWENTY

"You daddy, he doing okay?" Lulu asks after she sits between Lupé and Sue in her desk in our small circle.

"No, he's not." I lean forward. "Thank you for visiting him and bringing food." All three women have come to see my father twice now.

"You pray for Daddy?" Lulu asks.

I shake my head. The few times I prayed for my father out of desperation it didn't seem to work. "I did, but…I guess…I'm not very religious."

She reaches in the pocket of her blue shirt. A little silver cross appears between her thumb and index finger. Small chocolate-colored beads peek over the fold of her pocket, one after the other. I realize she's holding a rosary. She winds it on the desk into a double circle and places the cross in the middle.

"I'm not religious," I say again. I'm not sure these

women would understand if I told them I don't
believe in anything.

"Angel with Daddy," Lulu says, fingering the first
bead by the cross.

"What?"

She scrunches her forehead as if she's thinking
hard. "I...see...angel with Daddy."

"You did?" A weird sensation saturates my body,
makes my skin tingle.

"Jes. He no alone. Look like Daddy."

All three women nod.

"Did you see the angel, too?" I ask Lupé.

She shakes her head. "No, Lulu."

"Did you, Sue?"

"No."

"Angel with Daddy a lot," Lulu says.

"You saw an angel in my father's room?"

"Jes."

"In his room?" I blink, begin to feel numb.

She nods, looks very serious.

"Where?"

"Uh...by his..." She points to her head.

"An angel. Are you sure?" My head begins to
pound, the tips of my ears burn.

"Angel like Daddy. But little." She holds her thumb and index finger an inch apart.

They all nod again and I keep staring at them. "Little? You mean, a child?"

Lulu studies me for a moment, narrows her eyes. "No, like Daddy, but little."

I remember how my father thought someone was in his room the other day.

Lulu nods. "Angel there to take him."

"Take him?" I rub my forehead, confused. Are there angels that help people die? I have no idea, but these women seem so honest, caring, and I know they're not crazy.

"We pray." Lulu picks up the silver cross and the chocolate beads follow.

I'm supposed to be teaching English, not talking about my father, praying in a classroom. But I look at these women, the only people who have come to visit my father since he's been in my home, and I want to hug them for what they've done, how they care. They've brought food, thought about him, want to pray for him.

"Okay." I push my hands together. My palms are sweaty.

Lulu puts the rosary down, takes Sue's and Lupé's

hands. Lupé and Sue reach over and grasp my hands, and suddenly the four of us are connected.

They close their eyes. Lulu speaks in Spanish, stops, opens her eyes and looks at me.

"Sorry, English," she says.

"No, no, please say it in Spanish. It's okay, the words are so beautiful. Please. However you feel comfortable."

She begins again, her prayer lyrical, smooth. The words floating out of her mouth like baby birds leaving a small nest in late spring.

I close my eyes, let the softness of her voice flutter around me. I take a deep breath and, for the first time in months, I feel a bit of peace in my heart.

Our house glimmers with light, each window a yellow square that falls out onto the lawn and blends with winter moonlight. Usually when I come home from teaching, the house is dark, except for the family room where the TV throws shadows around the room.

I open the garage door, drive in and hurry out of the car. With all the lights on, something must be wrong. The family room looks odd, with the overhead light illuminating the area.

"David?" Worry races through my body.

"We're in here."

I round the corner into the living room. Dad is sitting in a wheelchair in his wrinkled blue pajamas. He looks up, smiles at me. David stands behind him with his hands on the metal handles.

"What are you doing?"

"Pushing your dad around the house. I wanted Stan to see something different. He's tired of the bedroom. Right, Stan?"

My father glances back at David, nods.

"Thought some new scenery might make him feel better."

David's voice is so full of hope.

"That's so nice of you."

"Stan had a little trouble with the wheelchair so I picked him up and put him in it." He pats the handles. "Right, Stan? You're getting a different view of the world tonight?"

"Yeah, the house looks good." Dad's lisp thickens each word.

Not so long ago, my father climbed mountains, built buildings, won awards. He drove long highways for days at a time, and was strong. I should be angry, but I'm not. Maybe Lulu's prayers helped me, or maybe it's just because I've started to accept our fate.

David smiles at me again and cups my father's shoulder. "We had a real good evening, didn't we, Stan?"

I smile, turn my head a little and realize I love my husband more than ever.

I'm standing in the doorway of Dad's bedroom. He's sleeping quietly. I know I should go to bed, but I'm sure I won't be able to sleep. An hour ago, David wheeled Dad back to his room and I helped my father get to the bathroom then into bed. Dad seemed so content to go to bed, so happy he'd spent time with David. Yet the deep fatigue in his gaze, the lines around his mouth, told me the evening wore him out.

His room has changed over the weeks—the hospital bed, the perpetual water glass on the night-stand, the hospice supplies sitting in the corner. Yet, now, moonlight showers the room, making the space look elegant.

I sit in the chair next to his bed. Muffled TV voices and David's laughter tumble down the hall, find me. I look at the space above the bed, where

Lulu said she saw the angel. All I see are shadows patterning against the white wall. I close my eyes, open them, want to see what Lulu sees. If I could, if a mystical occurrence would take place for me, I would believe again. If I could know my father would be okay, no matter what.

I sigh, press my hands together, but I only see tangled, shadowy lines.

Lulu is standing in our kitchen. It's 10:00 a.m. and, a moment ago I helped her carry two full grocery bags into the house from her car.

"I put food in re...fridg...er...a...tor?" she asks.

"No, I can do it later." I stretch my arm around her, hug her, then let go. "Go see Dad. He was so excited you were coming to visit. He's always so happy to see you, Lupé and Sue."

"They come later."

I watch her walk down the hall to his room then I begin unpacking one of the grocery bags. I have never been good at accepting gifts. I feel more comfortable giving. Today, Lulu has brought a ham, homemade potato salad, a coconut cake, more enchiladas. I stack everything in the refrigerator, except for the cake because there is no more room.

Lulu's soft prayerful Spanish words weave their way to me from my father's room.

At the kitchen window, I watch as patches of white clouds move across the sky, blocking the sunlight and creating shadows on the lawn. I wonder if Lulu is looking at the angel right now. My skin tingles a little. It must be comforting to have something to hold on to, to believe in.

I glance at the coconut cake still on the counter. It looks like one of the clouds outside, with its thick fluffy frosting. I lift the plastic cover, bring it close to my face. The coconut and sugar smell like the suntan lotion my mother rubbed on Lena and me the last summer our family was together. Lena and I lounged on blue beach towels, squinted at clouds, imagined pictures—a church with a steeple, a forest of trees.

On Saturdays, Dad came out, reached down and touched our hair, smiled. Then he told us the names of the wispy clouds. Lena would laugh and explain that she thought God put them in the sky—they were pictures just for us.

He'd shake his head, said we needed to think more scientifically—know clouds were formed by moisture.

I cut a huge piece of cake, put it on a white plate,

bring it to my nose and sniff. I can almost feel my father touching my hair. I eat bite after bite. At the window again, I squint as clouds glide by.

"Dad fine," Lulu says, bringing me back to the present. "He happy today." She stands at the edge of the room holding her rosary in her hand.

"The cake's so good." I hold up the empty plate, then put it in the sink with the fork. "Would you like a piece?"

"No, Sue made for you."

"Would you like coffee, a Coke, water?" I want to give her something, show her kindness in some way.

"Water. No cake." She touches her stomach, the rosary sways, and she laughs for a moment.

I get her a bottle of water from the refrigerator. *Re…fridg…er…a…tor.* An image of my father's happy expression surfaces and I smile.

"Dad loved coming to class. He got such a kick out of helping you, Sue and Lupé."

"We love Daddy."

In the family room, Lulu and I sit at opposite ends of the couch.

"Thank you for the food," I say, feel my heart opening up, the sadness I carry around most of the time melting away. There are newspapers stacked by

David's chair, magazines by the couch, papers I should have recycled days ago, and for a moment I feel embarrassed at how the house looks. I've always loved keeping a perfect house. But lately, I've been spending all my time in my father's room, and a neat house just doesn't seem important.

"I come help you." Lulu motions to the papers.

"Oh, no, I'll do it. It's just I like being with my dad. That's more important than cleaning the house."

"Jes. He need you."

"I need him, too." I think about how, while sitting in his room, I have questioned what I believe, how I crave something more to hold on to.

"I come Saturday, help you. Angel there today." She nods, looks so relaxed, as if she's announcing that the sun is out. "You see?"

I shake my head. "I've looked. I mean, I've really tried, but I haven't seen anything."

"Sometimes I no see. Then I—" she brings her hand to her chest, crosses herself "—pray. He come. Daddy talk to him today."

"My father is talking to the angel today, just a minute ago?"

"Jes." She turns her head a little, her expression growing even more serious. "Jes."

"What did he say?"

"Daddy say…" She shrugs her shoulders and her expression pinches, as if she's trying to figure out how to explain what he said. She shakes her head, smiles. "I no."

"Does he know who the angel is?"

"Jes."

"Did he call it by name?" My body begins to tingle more.

"Reeymond."

"Wait here." I get up, find the picture of Raymond that I dug out of the box last night when I couldn't sleep because all I could think about was how I don't want my father to die.

I come back, hand Lulu the picture. "Is this the angel?"

She turns the picture a little, squints.

"I think…" She shakes her head, then looks at me for a long time. "Jes, this angel." She crosses herself and places the picture on the coffee table. "Daddy okay. You need tell goodbye. He have angel now, he no need you no more."

"Tell him goodbye?"

"Jes. Daddy go to God. Angel take him there." She looks so hopeful, so truthful.

And I want to believe, trust the way she does, but I am not sure I can.

Lulu left fifteen minutes ago and I'm sitting in Dad's room. When she and the others walked into the classroom for the first time, I thought she would learn from me, but I'm realizing that it is the opposite. Her kindness, her trust in what she believes is an inspiration and fills me with wonder.

Before she left, she walked back to Dad's room, leaned over and kissed my father's forehead. Then she said "Goodbye, Daddy."

I explained to Dad that Lulu was going home, but she'd be back. He smiled, squeezed her hand and said, *Goodbye, Lulu*, his words thick and slow.

At the front door she hugged me, said she would come over on Saturday. I thought of arguing with her about helping me, but I just nodded. Then I watched her climb into her battered white Toyota Celica with the dented front left fender. She waved before she drove off.

Now Dad is lying on his left side, facing the window. The blinds are up and the room is bright with sunlight.

Tell goodbye.

As sick as he is, I don't want him to die. I want

my father to get better, but I know this won't happen.

I sit in-the chair by his bed, clasp my hands and stare at my father.

God, please help my father.

The back of his head still looks like Cary Grant's. I close my eyes and see my parents dancing around the dining room, laughing.

CHAPTER TWENTY-ONE

"Hello?" I say into the phone. I'm standing in the bedroom, next to the nightstand. It's eight-thirty and I'm still in my pajamas.

"Hi, this is Dr. London."

It seems like years since we've seen him. "Hello, how are you?" I sit on the edge of the bed.

"I was wondering if it would be okay if I visit your father in a few hours? I have to come out that way for a new patient and I thought I'd stop by."

"Of course. He'd love to see you. He doesn't get much company."

We set a time and I hang up, go into my dad's room.

"Dad?"

He opens his eyes, looks at me.

"Dr. London is coming to see you."

Confusion takes over his expression. "Who?"

His question stuns me. Every afternoon, I play

one of Dr. London's hypnosis tapes for Dad. He listens, and when it's over he always says, *I like Dr. London.*

"Dr. London. You know, your doctor, the one on the tape. He's coming here."

"That's good, honey. I like all the people here."

"All the people? You mean Lulu and Lupé?"

"All of them." He points to the left corner of the room and I look over to the corner and my heart begins to pound.

"There are people here?"

"Yeah."

I look around, turn back. He's always been so serious, so precise. He built strong buildings, told Lena and I not to believe in cloud pictures. And now...

"Who are they, Dad?"

He looks at me with surprise, then shrugs, closes his eyes as if he's so tired he can't say another word.

I'm standing in the kitchen, staring out the window. Dr. London is visiting Dad. Before he got here, I took a shower, pulled on jeans, a blue sweater, brushed my hair and dabbed on lip gloss. I want to be the same person I was months ago, before that first phone call from Dad. But I know there is no turning back.

Now I'm just holding on.

I hear Dr. London say goodbye to Dad. I walk into the living room, wait for him to come down the hall.

"It's really nice of you to visit my father," I say when he walks into the living room.

He nods, smiles, yet I see a deep sadness in his eyes.

I motion toward the couch. "Do you have time for coffee?"

"I'm fine." He sits on the couch and I take the other side. "I wanted to come, just sit with your father for a while."

"That's so thoughtful. I know you're busy."

"His nurse told me his progress, and I thought I'd better come out before it's too late."

I nod.

"I learned a lot from your father."

"You learned from Dad?" My question is a whisper, filled with surprise.

He nods.

"What did you learn?"

"He reminded me about what's really important. Sometimes I get so busy, I forget. The day he had to wait for me in my office, I apologized for running late. He told me that maybe one day I would be helping him and someone else would have to wait. To me, that's spirituality at its deepest—that pure understanding of how important it is to accept what we are given, realize there is a reason for everything."

A *reason for everything*.

"I'm still wrestling with why my father has to go through this, what could possibly be gained?" I ask.

"Maybe one day, you'll find out."

"I don't think I ever will. I thought for so long he was going to get better."

"Melinda, your father was very ill when he came to see me."

"But he did walk, and he came to my English class."

"It's good he got to do those things. He thinks a lot of you. I guess I should go. I'll try to come out again."

He stands and so do I. His expression is so sad, I have to turn away for a moment to gain control.

"I wish I could have done something more for your father."

"You did what you could," I say.

"I'll come back to see him."

"There probably won't be enough time." I know this is true, and I watch the sadness in his expression deepen. I put my arms around him, hug him, then gently kiss his cheek.

"You're a good person. You helped my father so much. He really likes you."

"Thanks."

A moment later I watch Dr. London walk to his car. Deep in my heart I know this is the last time I'll see him, and it's all right.

It's Wednesday morning.

David just left for work. I went out to the garage, kissed him goodbye, then watched as he pulled out. Our lives have slipped into this pattern—me taking care of my father, David going to work with a worried look on his face.

The house is quiet, peaceful, like a church before people file in. I walk down the hall, go into Dad's room and stand by the bed. He's lying on his back, his hands flat against his stomach.

"Dad."

He opens his eyes, blinks. "Hi."

"How are you?"

"Get everyone whatever they want."

I look behind me, then feel idiotic because I know I won't see anyone. I take his hand, rub his fingers.

"Honey, will you get those people something to eat and drink? Whatever they want." He stares over my shoulder as if he's looking at someone.

"What people?" My heart pounds faster.

"The people next to you. Right there."

"Who are they?"

"Mama, Daddy, Raymond." Then Dad looks directly at me, squeezes my hand. "They want me to go home. Is it okay if I go?"

The lisp softens the edges of his words.

"Dad, you…"

He looks at me calmly. "I need to go home, honey. I'm tired."

I rub his hand, know this is what Lulu was talking about. "Dad, go home if you need to."

His expression softens. "Thanks. They think I should go."

He closes his eyes and sighs. I stand very still. Dad breathes in a gentle rhythm. I pat his hand, look around the room. I see only white walls and the picture of the New Mexico church that I hung so long ago. I put the painting on the wall without much thought. The colors looked pretty in here, but I never anticipated that my father would be looking at it for so long, never thought this room would become our chapel.

It's six-thirty Thursday morning. Dad's breath is shallow and he won't wake up.

"Dad," I call again, shake his shoulder gently, but he doesn't open his eyes. The doorbell rings and I run to answer it. Elizabeth walks in, her face somber. I called her ten minutes ago.

"Any changes?"

I shake my head and she heads back to his room.

Standing in the bedroom doorway, I watch as she listens to his heart with her stethoscope, then takes his pulse. She turns around and the way she looks at me answers every question I have.

"He's in a coma."

I lean against the doorjamb. I want him to open his eyes, sit up and tell me he sees people I can't see. But I know he's worn out and so am I.

"I have other patients today, but I can get someone to cover for me and stay with you." She puts her stethoscope in her bag.

"Is there anything we can do?"

"There's really nothing anyone can do."

"We'll be fine." I don't want to be alone, but I know she has work to do, other people to care for. We walk out to the living room and Elizabeth hugs me. I feel the warmth of her body, her kindness.

"If you need me, I'm just a phone call away." She touches her cell on the waistband of her slacks.

"I know. I think we'll be okay. I was planning on trying to get him in his wheelchair today."

I look toward his room. The doorway is illuminated with a bright light—warm, beckoning.

"You won't be able to do that. He's dying, Melinda. You need to accept that."

I nod. "He told me last night he wants to go home. I knew then it wouldn't be long."

"You sure you're okay?"

"I'm fine."

She hitches her bag over her shoulder, opens the door. "It's warm out, like spring."

Like spring.

I walk out onto the porch. We stand close, arms around each other, looking out to the yard that is drenched with light.

"None of his friends came to see him. Except for my students."

"A lot of people are afraid, honey."

I take a step back, look at her. "He was always so nice to everyone. It's a shame they wouldn't come. He would have liked that."

"Sometimes people can't face the hard parts of life. But they miss a lot."

"Yeah." I look at the pansies, think about how my father said he wanted to see the daffodils bloom. "It always seems to take forever for spring to get here. And then, suddenly, it's here, and everything is okay."

We hug again and she is gone.

I sat in Dad's bedroom for most of the afternoon. He was breathing softly and the sound comforted me. A few moments ago I came into the kitchen to start dinner. I hear the garage open and I go to meet David.

My husband's expression changes to worry when he sees me standing by the door.

"Any changes?" he asks as he gets out of his car.

"No."

His mouth twists into a grim line. "Did Elizabeth come back?"

"No, there's nothing she can do. She said she'd come over early tomorrow morning."

David sighs, rubs his face, then walks around the cars, sets his briefcase down and puts his arms around me. His hug makes me feel safe and I realize we haven't hugged like this in years.

"I'm sorry," he says.

"I know." I look up at him. "Dinner's ready. You must be hungry."

"Not now."

He takes my hand and we walk into the house.

It's 6:00 a.m. A moment ago I woke with a start, thought I heard a noise like Dad had fallen out of bed again. The light coming from my father's room is so bright, I blink. I run down the hall, go in.

My father's eyes are closed. I look at his chest. There is no movement.

I walk over, take his hand. It's still warm.

I'm on the front porch, looking up at the dark sky, plump with rain clouds. The air is tense with coming rain. I expected a clear morning sky. I cross my arms, feel numb. Last night's rain slicked the oak branches, and even from here, I can see tiny green leaves have sprouted. The growth must have happened yesterday or the day before.

The front door opens and I turn.

"What are you doing out here?" David asks, comes onto the porch. "Aren't you cold?"

"I just wanted to see the morning. I didn't know it was about to rain." I close the space between us and wrap my arms around him.

"Dad's gone."

He leans back a little with a questioning look on his face.

"I called Elizabeth. She'll be right over."

David shakes his head, looks as if he's been slapped. "He's gone?"

I nod, hug him harder, begin to cry.

"Why don't you come inside? You should rest."

He leads me back into the house, to the living room couch. I sit, think that I need to pour a glass of milk for Dad, go back to his bright room and hold his hand.

But all that is over now.

Elizabeth left two hours ago. She handled all the arrangements. The funeral home came and got Dad's body. Now Lulu is here. She arrived at eight, like she said she would.

"You okay?" Lulu stops taking containers out of her grocery bag and looks at me, concern on her face.

"I'm okay." I walk over and put my arm around her. "Thank you for visiting my father."

"I like Daddy. He good man."

"I know." I stay next to her and rub my forehead. David is talking on the phone, calling people to tell them.

"You tired. Sit," Lulu says.

"I'm okay." I don't say that I want to be next to her, that I feel kindness and warmth from her, and I want to stay beside her because she is my friend, someone who knew how nice my father was.

"You daddy better off. He with my daddy. He teach him English."

I smile and she does, too.

"I didn't think of that."

"Oh, they there." She points to the ceiling. "My daddy teach your daddy Spanish." She crosses herself, then takes a baked chicken wrapped in plastic out of the grocery bag and puts it on the counter. The plastic is cloudy with moisture. She leans over and hugs me. "Everything be okay. You see."

David, Jennifer and I are on our way to the Fort Worth airport. I'm in the back seat and Jennifer is in the front with her father. I touch her long blond hair, feel the smooth silkiness of the strands.

She turns around, smiles at me.

"Your hair's pretty, so soft," I say.

"Oh, Mom, you always say that." But she smiles again. "You look tired. After you drop me at the airport, you need to go home and rest." She looks at her father. "Dad, make her rest. She needs to go to bed."

"I will."

My father's memorial was yesterday, in our backyard, where he walked. The afternoon was warm, still, and the sky was filled with soft, scattered clouds. Before the minister spoke, I turned my face to the sky, watched clouds float by. Elizabeth made arrangements for the hospice minister to come out, and he spoke about rebirth and spring—the cycle of life. Then everyone came inside and ate sandwiches that Lulu, Lupé and Sue made.

Jennifer hovered around me, brought me a plate of food and insisted I sit on the couch and rest. She cleaned up after everyone left, tucked a blanket around my legs. I was surprised at how good it felt to be taken care of by my daughter.

David talked to Lulu before she went home, and

I saw him give her money for all the three women had done. This gesture touched my heart so much. The only other people who came to the memorial were Elizabeth's husband, Brad, Deanne and Jim Smith. Of course I didn't expect anybody else. Yet I was hoping that someone from my father's life in Las Cruces would show up, but no one even sent a card.

David called Jan the morning Dad died. Then he phoned her again and let her know when the memorial would be. She said she couldn't possibly travel so far, that her heart was breaking and she didn't know what she was going to do without Stanley.

That was the last we heard from her.

And the Skillys? Mr. Skilly told David he and his wife were both too sick to fly.

I called my sister after David had made all the other calls. She promised she would come for the memorial, but yesterday morning at 5:00 a.m., she told me she was suffering from a migraine. I started to get angry, but I imagined what my father would say to me, how he would explain she had a rough beginning, and I should understand that. So I told Lena it was all right, that Dad would understand. And so did I.

Jenny came home the day before yesterday. David and I picked her up at the airport. When she walked into baggage claim, she looked so pretty and grown-up in her hiphugger jeans and pink sweater. The minute I saw her, I started to cry. I stood in awe of her gentle beauty as she walked over to us. In the months she's been away, her lovely face, with her incredibly slanted eyes, has matured. She is blooming into a woman, and the little girl I knew has faded.

Today she's flying back to school because it's midterm week and she can't miss it. I want her to stay but as Elizabeth said, as much as we sometimes don't want it to, life moves on.

David pulls into a parking space at the C Terminal. We climb out of the car and he gets Jenny's small bag from the back seat.

"I'll get it, Dad," she says, takes the handle from his hand. "It's not heavy."

"You're the boss, punkin'." It's a name we have called her since the day she was born. He hugs her. "Thanks for helping your mother."

I look at the sky. It is a beautiful blue, clear, and the air is crisp, full of March surprises.

"You *are* coming home for Easter?" I ask as I put my arm around her and we begin walking across the street to the airport terminal. "It's late this year, in April. I promise we'll eat lots of jellybeans."

"I was thinking about going to Mexico with some friends." She gives me a cajoling smile. "I'll be fine, Mom. There's a whole group that's going."

I brush away the worry, feel happy for her. I want her to have a fun, full life with lots of memories.

"Okay, go, but you'll have to call me every night."

David comes up beside us. "My vote is she shouldn't go. But we can discuss this later. Right now she needs to get through security."

Jennifer turns and wraps her arms around me.

"I'm sorry about Grandpa. It's weird. Last night I was thinking, I mean, where did he go?" She leans back and I see tears and hurt in her blue eyes.

"I believe your grandfather's spirit is still with us. He was so sick. I know it hurts, but he's better off." I want her to believe this, to feel comforted by what happened to my father.

I gently take her beautiful face between my hands, kiss her cheek and remember the tiny image I saw in my dream twenty years ago. How hopeful and happy I was that morning knowing I was having a little girl. I wondered who she would be, wished the best for her. And now, here she is, a young woman with dreams and hopes of her own, and I'm happy.

"We did good," David says as she walks through the metal detector. He puts his arm around me when she picks up her bag from the X-ray machine, turns and smiles that wonderful smile.

Third Week in April

I'm sitting in Dad's room. The hospital bed is gone and the room looks like it did before our journey began. Afternoon sunlight is rushing in, adding a familiar glow to the room. I miss my father so much sometimes, my chest aches with grief. But I know it will fade with time, with our lives moving forward.

Yesterday, Rebecca called and asked me to take a permanent position with the school district. They are enlarging their English as a Second Language program and she wants me to teach more classes, help her expand it. A few moments ago I called her and accepted the position.

My father would be happy about this.

After I hung up the phone, I came in here. Deep down I was hoping to see the angel Lulu saw, or the people Dad talked about, but there are no signs, nothing except crystal sunlight painting the walls.

I haven't told anyone this, but sometimes late in the afternoon when I'm standing in the kitchen or sitting in the family room, I think I hear my father call my name. I tell myself it's just my imagination, yet there is a part of me—the part that now believes in things I can't see, that knows my father is close by. So I come back here and I am filled with hope.

I get up, walk down the hall and open the front door. Spring sunshine tumbles in, fills the space, surrounds me with light. At the oak tree that is lush with new leaves, I kneel down and feel the soft grass against my bare legs.

Around the tree base the beginnings of my daffodils are peeking through the dark earth, their fragile stems anxious for warmth and life. It seems so long ago that I held the hard bulbs in my hands, wasn't sure they would grow. Soon the flowers will be tall, circling the tree, raging with beauty, my father's gift to me.

They were twin sisters with nothing in common…

Until they teamed up on a cross-country
adventure to find their younger sibling.
And ended up figuring out that, despite
buried secrets and wrong turns, all roads
lead back to family.

Sisters

by Nancy Robards Thompson

Available June 2006
TheNextNovel.com

HN46

Hearing that her husband
had owned a cottage in England
was a surprise. But the truly
shocking news was what
she would find there.

Determined to discover more about the cottage
her deceased husband left her, Marjorie Maitland
travels to England to visit the property—and
ends up uncovering secrets from the past that
might just be the key to her future.

The English Wife

by Doreen Roberts

HN47

HARLEQUIN®
Next™

REQUEST YOUR FREE BOOKS!

2 FREE NOVELS TO INTRODUCE YOU TO OUR BRAND-NEW LINE!

There's the life you planned. And there's what comes next.

There comes a time in every woman's life when she needs more.

Sometimes finding what you want means leaving everything you love. Big-hearted, warm and funny, Flying Lessons is a story of love and courage as Beth Holt Martin sets out to change her life and her marriage, for better or for worse.

Flying Lessons

by

Peggy Webb

Available May 2006
TheNextNovel.com

HN42

It's a dating jungle out there!

Four thirtysomething women with
a fear of dating form a network of
support to empower each other as they
face the trials and travails of modern
matchmaking in Los Angeles.

The I Hate To Date Club

by
Elda Minger

Is reality better than fantasy?

When her son leaves for college, Lauren realizes it is time to start a new life for herself. After a series of hilarious wrong turns, she lands a job decorating department-store windows. Is the "perfect" world she creates in the windows possible to find in real life? Ready or not, it's time to find out!

Window Dressing

by Nikki Rivers